"You could do worse than marry a Manxman."

As Juan spoke, Nora looked up, startled. "Are you telling me this is on your own behalf? That someone will get a prize if they marry *you*?"

Juan threw back his head and laughed. "Lord, no! But there's always Jony," he paused and smiled wickedly. "No doubt he'll find time for you."

She quivered. "You make me feel like some rich heiress who could be held for ransom!"

Juan raised an eyebrow. "You mean like someone abducting you to force you into marriage in order to share your inheritance?"

Rich color swept over her and she said, "Charming! Nice to know that I need money to boost my sex appeal!"

"You don't need anything," he said as he pulled her close. Then his mouth closed over her own trembling one.

Other titles by
KATRINA BRITT
IN HARLEQUIN ROMANCES

Other titles by
KATRINA BRITT
IN HARLEQUIN PRESENTS

Many of these titles are available at your local bookseller.

For a free catalogue listing all available Harlequin Romances,
send your name and address to:

HARLEQUIN READER SERVICE,
M.P.O. Box 707, Niagara Falls, N.Y. 14302
Canadian address: Stratford, Ontario N5A 6W2

Island
for Dreams

by

KATRINA BRITT

Harlequin Books

TORONTO • LONDON • LOS ANGELES • AMSTERDAM
SYDNEY • HAMBURG • PARIS • STOCKHOLM • ATHENS • TOKYO

Original hardcover edition published in 1980
by Mills & Boon Limited

ISBN 0-373-02371-5

Harlequin edition published December 1980

CHAPTER ONE

NORA came to the island when the yellow gorse was
in full bloom and the blue, blue sea edged with
snowy white foam was topped by the billowing sails
of yachts beneath a shimmering blue sky. The first
glimpse of one of the United Kingdom's most beautiful offshore islands was enough to halt the light-
hearted chatter of the passengers at the end of an
hour-long flight from London.

Attention was drawn on the lush green fields
sparkling in the crystal clean air immediately below the hovering wing tips of the plane as it came in
to land.

'Beautiful and peaceful, isn't it?' remarked the
elderly woman seated next to Nora. 'Like another
world after the polluted and overcrowded cities on
the mainland. I adore the Isle of Man.' The woman
turned a neatly lacquered hair-do to take a closer
look at the slender silent girl beside her. 'On holiday?'

Nora smiled and shook her head. 'Not really.'

'Combining business with pleasure, eh? There's
nothing like it, especially if you happen to be young
and pretty. You are lucky.'

Nora leaned back in her seat and closed her eyes.
The woman could be right. She was lucky in a way,
if material things were anything to go by, like the
legacy which had brought her to the island. But she
would have gladly given everything she had to have
her parents back again.

Orphaned at twenty—her parents had been
killed outright in a road accident—she had stag-

7

gered through the following months of grief with a youthful dignity and courage which had helped her to go on running the family business as if her father was still there. Being his typist had helped and this along with her vivid imagination, foresight and stamina, had taken her to the top. At the end of four years she had passed her exams and was firmly established as a qualified land and estate agent.

Of medium height, small-boned and neatly made with a cloud of fair hair, and melting brown eyes, she looked appealingly fragile and very misleading. By nature Nora was robust and healthy, with an attractive husky voice and moderate tastes. Her intelligence covered a wide field and her conversation, along with her appearance, was appealing to men.

Success, however, had not gone to her head. She had friends of both sexes and was popular because she could be trusted and was also decorative at parties. Despite the number of proposals she had received Nora was in no hurry to get married.

She admitted a fondness for her cousin Floyd whom she had taken on as a partner in the business, but that was all. Her one regret was that she had never met Jed Kelly, whose death was her reason for coming to the island.

Jed Kelly had been in love with her mother and he had never forgotten her when she had married an Englishman and gone to live on the mainland. He had never married and Nora had not known that he existed until she was notified of his will. She was to share his estate with a man named Jony Cesar, his son by adoption.

'Miss Bain?'

Nora had collected her case and was walking towards the airport exit when the man stepped in front of her. She saw a man who looked to be in his thirties with lean Celtic features, small dark eyes and brown hair. Of medium height, he gave the impression of broadness and strength.

She nodded and said with a smile, 'You must be Jony Cesar.'

'That's right.' His voice, like his expression, was deadpan. 'I hardly expected you to be so young.'

'I'm twenty-four.'

He raised a surly brow. 'I can give you a few years,' he admitted without enlarging upon it. 'This all your luggage?'

He took her case and she walked beside him out of the airport to a waiting car.

'I suppose you knew Mr Kelly well,' she said. 'I hope you'll tell me a lot about him.'

He shrugged. 'There isn't much to tell. I reckon you're lucky that he left his affairs in order, even to preparing an apartment for you on the sea front at Ramsey in the north of the island.'

Nora watched him place her case in the trunk of the car, then open the door of the front seat for her to get in.

'He didn't expect me to live here permanently, did he?' she asked as he slipped into the driving seat beside her.

'He was hoping that you would marry a Manxman,' he replied, setting the car in motion.

They drove off in silence and gradually Nora forgot the surliness of her companion in the beauty of her surroundings. The forecourt of the air terminal with its velvet lawns, colourful flower beds and palm trees whispering in the breeze was picturesque and welcoming under a very blue sky.

Green fields came into view dotted with black and white cattle, then sheep. Nora sat up with a cry of pleasure at the sight of them.

'Oh! Baby lambs!' she cried. 'Aren't they sweet?

You mustn't take any notice of me—I usually go gooey-eyed over anything young and cuddly.'

Her companion, however, neither turned his head nor spoke, but Nora was staring straight ahead now with shining eyes and pink parted lips, taking in the notice by a small stone bridge.

'The Fairy Bridge!' she cried. 'Isn't one supposed to say something? Like, "Hello, fairies"?'

'You've said it as we were passing over the bridge,' he replied, keeping his eyes on the road.

Nora's hands, clasped loosely in her lap, trembled a little. One did not have to be clairvoyant to see that this stranger was not exactly putting out the red carpet for her.

She glanced sideways at her taciturn companion. 'I noticed that you didn't greet the fairies.' He shrugged and her soft mouth tightened. 'Is it the fairies whom you've no time for or me?' she asked.

'I'm not against you personally,' he admitted grudgingly. 'It's just that I think old Jed must have been out of his mind to split the estate up.'

'You mean you think you ought to have had everything?'

'Not exactly, but it would have been better just to leave you some money. I can't see what good it's going to do you coming over here. You do know the terms of the will, don't you?'

'No, I don't. I'm supposed to be seeing the lawyer when I arrive,' she answered. 'Do you?'

Again he shrugged. 'Part of them. Better let the lawyer tell you.'

'You mean there are strings attached?' she asked apprehensively.

'Better wait until you've seen the lawyer. I'm taking you to him now.'

Nora noticed his clothes then, the leggings and gear of a farmer. He had not even changed to meet her, she thought, then immediately dismissed the thought as unworthy since he could be spending time he could ill afford away from his work.

'Are you a farmer?' she asked.

'Yes. Jed left me the farm and bought you the apartment. We share all the land between us.'

'The land?' she queried.

'There's plenty of it around the island. Not immediately round the farm, that's mine, but there are acres and acres on outlying farms that Jed lets out to them on a lease.'

'But why did he not sell the farmers the land?'

'Because he said they had enough and he hated speculators. Jed was afraid that whoever bought the land would sell it to speculators to build on.'

Nora said softly and gently, 'He must have loved the island. You wouldn't sell to speculators, would you?'

The answer obviously required much thought, because Jony Cesar was a long time answering.

At last he said slowly, 'I couldn't very well without your consent.'

Nora looked at him aghast. 'You can't sell to speculators if Mr Kelly was so much against it, surely? Besides, he might have made that a condition in his will.'

'There are always ways and means of getting over these things,' he replied.

The lawyer resided in the hilly part of Douglas, the bustling capital of the island. A shrewd elderly man, he came right to the point when Nora had established her identity. As Jony had said earlier, the farm had been left to him and the flat to Nora, with the monies from the land and other investments to be divided between them.

It was the last condition in the will that finally took Nora's breath away. She was to marry a Manxman if single at the time of her benefactor's death; only then could she inherit. She was still shaken about it when, the interview over, she was again sitting in the car with Jony.

The lawyer had been very kind and had advised her to contact him if she had any problems. He reminded her that the flat was her own, had given her the keys and had promised to get in touch at a later date to hand over the deeds.

'But why should Mr Kelly insist that I marry a Manxman?' She made a helpless gesture with her hands and spoke almost to herself, and gave her companion an exasperated look.

'Are you married?' she asked curiously.

'No. Never got around to it.'

'Don't you find it lonely?'

'No. I get around...pubs mostly...play darts, go fishing, that sort of thing.' He favoured her with a glance. 'You can get round that marrying a Manxman by marrying one and later divorcing him.'

Nora gazed at him in astonishment. 'I'd never dream of such a thing! You're very devious, aren't you? I don't mean that as an insult, but you seem to have an answer for just about everything.'

'That's the way to be if you want anything in this world. Take old Jed, for instance, he never went anywhere in the way of company, neither did he entertain at his home. He had a shrewd eye for making money which he's left for someone else to spend.'

'You should be grateful to him for leaving you so much. As for me, I don't know what I'm going to do yet.'

'You could stay at the flat for a while and look around the island.'

They were going along the coast road now, with panoramic views of the sea at every bend in the road. On their right white villas clung to the slopes, on their left cattle and sheep grazed in the fields.

The rich golden gorse lined the hedgerows and decorated the fields in huge bouquets, and Nora fell in love with Laxey, nestling in the feet of the cliffs where houses of Manx stone rubbed shoulders with new villas in a picturesque haphazard fashion.

Leaving Laxey behind, they took the coast road again with a view of the famous Laxey wheel to their left and on to Ramsey.

Jony dropped her off at the promenade entrance to her flat overlooking the sea. It was on the top floor of a three-storey block with panoramic views. It was a relief for Nora to be on her own, for Jony's company, in her opinion, left much to be desired. Perhaps he did not like girls, she thought, opening the door of her flat, then promptly forgetting all about him.

The flat was small and compact with the verandahed lounge and two bedrooms on the front overlooking the water. The kitchen, toilet, bathroom and linen cupboards were on the inside of the building, with air-conditioning instead of windows. French windows opened on to the verandah, and as a delighted Nora explored her smile became fixed.

The refrigerator was stocked with food, as were the wall cupboards. There was a crusty fresh loaf in the bread bin and a bottle of milk with half a dozen fresh eggs in the refrigerator. Whoever had furnished the kitchen with all the necessities had done an excellent job and she was very grateful. She toyed with the idea that it could not have been a man.

She thought it could hardly be Jony; it was more likely to be someone the lawyer had sent to do the job. She hummed softly to herself as she made an omelette from fresh eggs from the fridge and

resolved to discover whom she had to thank for
everything in the flat.

She carried her meal on to the little balcony and
gazed out over the sea as she ate contentedly. Strange
that the conditions of the will had not upset her as
much as Jony Cesar had with his brusque, almost
rude manner.

Thinking about him, Nora felt an emotion not
unlike anger blocking her throat. He was a man,
with a male's viewpoint of Jed Kelly's will. He was
too uncouth, if that was the word, ever to be a
friend. Women might be an unknown quantity in
his tight little world. In any case why bother with
such a man? She could deal outright with the
lawyer.

The sound of a motorboat drew her eyes once
more to the beach on the far side of the promenade to
the flat. The tide was in and a red motorboat was
some distance away in the sea towing a water-skier.

The skier was a girl in a red bathing suit. They were
too far away for Nora to see their features, but she
could see the young man in the boat had black rough
curly hair, was broad-shouldered and looked strong.
She saw the red motorboat again later as she took a
walk before going to bed.

The lovely July evening beckoned and Nora
crossed the promenade and went down on the
beach. Her only companions were the lovely white-
breasted seagulls poking in puddles in the sand left
by the tide for their supper. Walking along the
water's edge she passed under the iron supports of
the pier to continue along the beach, and there was
the red motorboat again towing the girl in the red
swimsuit.

The girl had a perfect figure and she handled the
skis expertly, Nora noticed before giving her attention to the man in the motorboat. His face was

tanned and his teeth, as he shouted something over his shoulder at the girl in tow, were startlingly white.

They made one more circle of the water, then they were gone. Nora strolled along and looked up the beach to see the bank of pebbles washed up by the tide against the sea wall. Above the wall green slopes led up to the long cream building of the Beach Hotel.

Retracing her steps, Nora picked up strange shells, some of which were a pinky pearl and almost transparent. There were coloured stones too which could be made into jewellery. She pocketed some of the bigger shells and several of the stones and realised that she was feeling pleasantly tired. And there remained the niggling question of what she was to do about the terms of the will.

No doubt Jony was hoping that she would not follow out the terms of the will and so leave him to inherit everything. Well, she might do just that, but tomorrow was time enough to think about it.

In the pristine freshness of her bedroom Nora undressed and prepared for bed. It had been quite a day and the cool sheets had never been so welcome.

Her problems came back in force when she awakened next morning to the cry of seagulls on the shore. Padding across the carpet, she looked out over a sea covered by early morning mist. Some distance along the promenade a man was putting scraps out for the seagulls and they were wheeling and screeching excitedly above his head.

Down below the tide was going out and the beach lay golden and inviting and fresh. Lifting her arms above her head, Nora stretched luxuriously. She was going to enjoy her visit to the island, Jony or no Jony, and with this thought in mind she turned, humming to herself, and made her way with a light step to the bathroom.

She had finished her breakfast and was making coffee when her door bell rang.

'Good morning,' said Jony as she opened the door. 'I called to see how you were going on. I didn't think you would be up so early.'

'Oh, good morning,' Nora gasped, taken aback by her unexpected visitor. 'Come in. I'm just making coffee.'

Jony stepped inside awkwardly. 'Nice place you have here,' he remarked, looking admiringly at the gold wall-to-wall carpet and matching silk curtains at the windows of the lounge.

He was studying two watercolours of the island on the main wall when Nora came from the adjoining kitchen with coffee.

'I wondered where these had gone,' he said gruffly. 'They used to be at the farm—Jed must have had them brought here. I had my eye on them. I was hoping they would be mine.'

'Really?' Nora poured out the coffee. 'Black or white?' she asked.

'Black, please.'

Jony lowered himself with an ill grace into one of the two easy chairs by the French windows and accepted his drink. He wore a dark blue suit and pale blue shirt and his hair had stood for a good deal of brushing.

Nora sat down on the settee beneath the two watercolours and sipped her coffee.

She asked, 'Did you have anything to do with stocking up my larder and kitchen? I'm very grateful for it.'

He shook his head. 'Jed arranged everything with his lawyer. He was hoping to see you in the flat before he died, but it wasn't to be.'

Nora blinked back the tears. 'Poor Mr Kelly!'

She gazed at him curiously with the feeling that this was another aspect of the man that she had not met. It was clear to her now that he was out to please.

Bluntly, she asked, 'Why this early visit? As a farmer I would have thought you'd be at one of the busiest parts of the day now.'

'I have the day off. Got a man in,' he replied, reaching for a biscuit she had placed on a plate. 'This coffee isn't bad.'

'And why have you taken the day off work?' she insisted.

'Thought you'd like to see a bit of the island.'

She asked, 'Was Mr Kelly buried or cremated? I'd like to put some flowers on his grave.'

'Cremated,' Jony answered laconically, and reached for a second biscuit. 'Where would you like to go?'

Nora put down her empty cup and leaned back in her chair.

'I'm not aiming at going anywhere today,' she admitted frankly. 'I'm just going to take things nice and easy.' She stretched out long slim legs in slacks and smiled at him. 'Sorry.'

'Got another date?'

'No. It's just that I like time before I go out with anyone. Why the sudden interest? Yesterday you gave the impression that not only were you not interested but that you couldn't wait to be rid of me.'

He mumbled sheepishly, 'I was a bit out of my depth. I never expected anyone like you.'

'Was that what it was?' Her dainty eyebrows shot up in disbelief. Then she smiled impishly. 'You thought that because I was a miss, I was some frumpish old maid eager for the legacy?'

His look at her was so surprised that Nora guessed she had been very near the truth.

Doggedly, he said, 'I had my own ideas like everyone else. Everyone will be surprised when they see you.'

'Everyone? You mean Mr Kelly's family or yours?'

'Jed has no family and mine hardly count. I mean the people here in Ramsey will all be wanting to have a look at the girl Jed has left part of his money to.'

Nora was aghast. 'But surely no one knows yet? I mean, the conditions of the will and so on.'

He shook his head and gave her a pitying look. 'You don't know the half of it. They probably all know by now about this flat, what it was stocked with for you and what money you'll receive, take it or leave it, to the last pound or so.'

Nora put back her head and laughed huskily. 'How lovely! I think I'm going to like it here very much.'

Again the stare of disbelief. 'You don't care what people are saying about you?'

She shook her head. 'Why should I? It's nice of them to be so concerned. I might find out quite a bit about my benefactor.'

'Oh, well,' Jony shrugged, putting down his cup, 'if you're going snooping around ...'

'What do you mean by snooping? Have you got something to hide or something?'

'Of course I haven't. So you're not coming out with me today?'

Nora had the feeling that he was being tolerant against his will.

'Sorry. Some other time, perhaps.'

He took his dismissal calmly and paused at the door.

'You shouldn't have much difficulty in marrying a Manxman. You're pretty enough to have your choice.'

Nora smiled. 'I reckon that's very noble of you. But I shouldn't let it worry you—I'm in no hurry to get married. Be seeing you!'

When he had gone Nora leaned back against the closed door. Slowly a smile crept over her face. Her sojourn on the island was going to be anything but dull, by the looks of it. Pity about Mr Kelly being cremated, though, she thought soberly. It would have kind of evened things up a bit if she could have taken some flowers to his grave by way of saying thank you.

To her way of thinking it was positively indecent to feel so happy and carefree about her legacy when it had come to her because of her benefactor's death. But there it was, and he had evidently wanted her to enjoy it, since he had gone to such pains in planning the whole thing. All of which reminded her to telephone his lawyer to thank him.

Richard Garrant sounded surprised but pleased that she should thank him for carrying out the wishes of his late client. He was touched by her thoughtfulness and reminded her that he was there to help her at any time.

There was a shopping precinct directly behind the flats, Nora discovered when she went out for fresh milk and bread. The day was sunny and warm, the tide was coming in lazily beneath a blue sky and the wooden pier beckoned.

Nora strolled along it after doing her shopping and leaned over the pier rail at the far end to watch several yachts putting out to sea. She had tied a scarf around her hair as a protection from the sea breeze, but being silk it had worked loose. The next moment it had fallen from her hair to sail downwards to the water, and she watched it with dismay as it went out of sight beneath the pier.

Running down the steps leading down to the beach now submerged by the tide, she saw it wrapped around one of the girders supporting the pier not far from where she was standing.

Nora was in no fit state to reason. The scarf had been one of the last presents she had received from her parents before they had been killed. To lose it was unthinkable. She was aggravatingly near to reaching it, but not quite near enough. If only her arms had been a bit longer! she thought desperately, stretching herself out to the full limit.

One last desperate lunge and it happened. Losing her balance, Nora fell into the water. Just before she plunged she thought she heard someone call, but could not recall seeing anyone apart from a boat anchored to a buoy some distance from the pier.

It was the work of seconds to snatch the scarf from its resting place before she made for the pier steps again. By the steps was a small dinghy with a lone occupant when she clambered on to them dripping wet.

'Lady,' drawled a deep voice, 'was it necessary to do the rescue act for a mere scarf?'

Nora straightened, dashed the soggy wet hair from her streaming face and favoured the man with a withering look. With the sea water trickling dismally down her back and front, and blinking the water from her eyes, she looked at the speaker. He had evidently come from the yacht anchored by the buoy.

There was something familiar about the dark crispy curling hair beneath the yachting cap, the lean tanned features, and the powerful breadth of shoulder in the polo-necked sweater. It was the man in the red motorboat of the previous evening who had been towing the girl.

'Sentimental reasons. It was a present from someone I loved very much,' she said coldly.

'Oh, come now! He wasn't worth all that effort, surely?'

The deep mocking voice held impatient undertones as he surveyed her dripping figure. He stood up in the rocking dinghy and it would have given her the greatest pleasure to see him lose his balance and plunge overboard.

'Yes, he was. My mother too, and I can't see what it has to do with you!'

She watched his changing expression as he reached out a powerful arm.

'Come with me,' he commanded in the tones of one who was used to being obeyed. 'You must get out of those wet things as quickly as possible.'

By now Nora, whose teeth were already chattering, could not have agreed more. Without question she took his outstretched hand and let him almost lift her into the dinghy. The next moment they were skimming over the water to the chug of the outboard motor and making straight for the anchored sloop. The man had stripped off his polo-necked sweater and pulled it over her head.

Nora could feel the heat from the sweater easing the clammy impact of her soggy clothes against her body. Part of her quivering was due to the situation which she now found herself in. Here she was speeding towards a boat with a complete stranger who could be for all she knew some kind of nut or sex maniac.

But the man had no idea of her dark thoughts as he lifted her aboard his boat.

'Welcome to the *Dancing Belle*,' he said with a grin as he let his hands linger on her trim waist.

Nora managed a quivering smile and followed him down a short ladder from the cockpit of the boat into the saloon. The sense of roominess had surprised her as they had descended through a large fibreglass hatch in the coach-roof which pushed forward, leaving the after-part of the saloon open to the sky above.

Two large non-opening windows gave plenty of light in headroom that was well over six feet. Her companion could just about stand upright.

'Not bad, is it?' he remarked, dwarfing the considerable roominess with his height and breadth of shoulder. 'Two quarter berths, one well over six feet and the other just under, tuck back beneath the cockpit side seats and this seat here is adjacent to the galley area. Been on a boat before?'

She shook her head and felt the water trickle down her back. Quelling a shudder, she said, 'Not a yacht. It's very nice. I suppose it moves pretty fast?'

She did not want to look at him, but he was the kind of man who demanded attention. Nora had never felt her sex more keenly than at that moment, and she wanted desperately to go back to the flat.

She did not want to look at him. Even so she was uneasily aware of rippling muscles beneath a skin of bronze satin. He had not been wearing anything beneath the polo-necked sweater which he had discarded for her and his powerful chest was dark and hirsute.

Then with a start she was aware of his dark eyes on her face.

'Better get out of those wet things as soon as possible,' he said. 'Shan't be a tick.'

He turned to go towards the galley, but she stopped him.

'I'd rather go home to change, if you don't mind,' she said primly.

He gave her a friendly grin. 'Be ruled by me, little one,' he told her. 'Get out of those things now—less risk of a chill.'

He disappeared into the galley, and Nora wondered how many girls he had entertained on the boat before her. He certainly was calm and cool about it. She could imagine girls making passes at him by the score. He was that type. Well, he would take no liberties with her!

She was still standing where he had left her and she was only conscious of the tall bronzed figure coming back. Above the frightened beating of her heart she saw his dark eyes narrow and a frown crease his forehead.

'Not started disrobing yet?' he teased. 'Come on, this won't do, you know.'

'You...you mean...I'm to undress right here?' she gasped.

He laughed, a deep chuckle that struck her quivering heart.

'Of course,' he replied in such a normal way as to make her feel ridiculous. 'Don't worry, I shall be too busy in the galley making a hot drink to see you. I'll pull the curtain across.'

He tossed two clean fluffy towels, another polo-necked sweater and pants at her.

'They're all freshly laundered,' he assured her. 'The clothes will be miles too big for you, but that isn't important. What is important is giving yourself a brisk rub down first.'

When he had gone Nora hastily peeled off her wet clothes and rubbed herself quickly with the towel, all the while keeping her frightened eyes on the curtain covering the galley.

She could hear him whistling and relaxed visibly when the sound of it came no nearer. Thoughtfully, she had put one towel to stand on to catch the dripping water, and also to place her wet clothes on when discarded.

The whistling had stopped when glowing from a brisk rub down, Nora gathered up the wet things in the towel to go tentatively towards the galley. She could hear the kettle almost on the boil, then suddenly the man was there.

He had changed into a cream woollen shirt and dark slacks. His firm mouth quirked with amusement at her appearance, at the loose sweater almost drowning her and the slacks which she had to hold up with one hand.

'I never thought my clothes could look so glamorous,' he commented. 'I'll take those wet things and roll them in a towel before putting them out to dry. If you go down that tiny corridor you'll find the washroom fixed up with a mirror if you want to comb your hair.'

Nora passed a deep hanging wardrobe under a shelf and right opposite to this behind a folding door was the washroom. There was a marine toilet and a plastic washbasin fitted with a mirror. Nora rooted in her shoulder bag for her make-up and combed her hair.

When she emerged still holding up the trousers, he was waiting with a piece of cord which he placed around her waist as her hair brushed his chin. He tied it in front with swift impersonal movements so that the few moments of his close proximity could not possibly have given offence.

'That's better.' He smiled down at her. 'Not much around the waist, are you? I can span it easily with my hands. Come on, I've made a drink.'

Nora was not sure whether her giddy reaction was due to his nearness or to the feeling of fright which was not, as yet, diminishing. The dinette was opposite the galley and she entered on wobbly legs.

The table stood on one single tubular leg with stowage space beneath its top for spare charts and a drawer beneath the base. The seats were upholstered in comfortable foam in orange to match the curtains.

Nora sat down, feeling more relaxed. Her companion was behaving like a gentleman up to now. She liked his deep cultured voice, the direct gaze of his dark eyes meeting her own rather wary ones full on, and his courtesy.

'I think it's time we introduced ourselves.' He was there with a tray containing freshly made coffee and thick slices of fruit cake. 'Juan Cregeen at your service.'

'Nora—Nora Bain.'

'Coffee black or white, Miss Bain? It is Miss, isn't it?' The dark intelligent eyes took in her ringless left hand.

'That's right. White coffee, please—and call me Nora.' She smiled up at him feeling very peculiar. 'May I call you Juan?'

He grinned. 'But certainly. Help yourself to sugar.'

He pushed a cut glass bowl containing brown sugar across the table to her and gave her a plate on which to put her fruit cake.

'Are you here on your own?' he asked politely.

'Yes.'

'On holiday?'

'Sort of.'

He sat down opposite her at the table and spooned sugar into his coffee.

'Not very forthcoming, are you? You're young to be on holiday alone,' he commented drily.

'I'm twenty-four,' she volunteered.

'I'm twenty-nine. Help yourself to cake. Arrive yesterday?'

'Yes, I saw you last night towing a girl in a red swim suit around the bay.'

He laughed, said lazily, 'Ah yes—Tricia. Not bad, is she?'

'You mean in looks or prowess?'

Nora helped herself to a piece of the fruitcake. Her dive in the sea had sharpened her appetite and the cake looked good.

'Her performance on the water-skis, of course. I've been teaching her.'

Nora wondered what else he had been teaching the absent Tricia and found herself resenting the girl.

Juan ignored the cake and drank his coffee. 'Rumour has it that you're here concerning a will. You'll discover in a very short time that it's impossible to keep anything dark in a place like Ramsey.'

Nora nearly choked on a morsel of cake. 'Did you know Mr Kelly?'

'No, but I know Jony Cesar—a wily character if ever there was one.'

She felt the hot colour rush beneath her clear skin and said indignantly, 'I suppose you know all about the will too.'

'That you have to marry a Manxman to inherit part of the money?'

Nora pushed the rest of her cake away, having lost her appetite.

She said tightly, 'I have a sneaky feeling that you knew all about me before you met me.'

He grinned, and reached in his breast pocket for cigarettes.

'Do you smoke?' he asked.

'Not very often.'

'Have one now. It will help you to relax.'

He offered her the open packet and took a lighter from the pocket of his trousers.

'Any friends here, or relations?' he asked, sitting back in his seat after lighting their cigarettes and exhaling smoke.

'I don't think so. Mother was Manx, but she went to the U.K. when she married.'

'Then you could do with a friend,' he said coolly. 'Will I do? To begin with, I could take you out for dinner this evening.'

Nora felt her face go hot. A few moments ago she had began to look upon this stranger as someone who was to be trusted. Now she was not too sure. He was behaving in the subtle way of all wolves who were suave and charming in stalking their prey.

She knew less than nothing about him and he had no kind word to say about Jony. Though what he said about Jony could be true, if her own opinion of the man was anything to go by. She bit her lip nervously. To be fair, she had not really felt alarmed at being on the boat with him, only wary. She was still going to be wary.

'Sorry, I can't see you this evening...I've made other plans. Some other time, perhaps.'

He lifted powerful shoulders. 'As you wish.' He leaned forward to tap the ash from his cigarette on to an ash tray on the table as Nora noted with dismay that her ash had fallen from her nervous holding of her cigarette on to the table.

Perhaps he had noticed it, hence his own action in tapping the ash from his own cigarette on to the ashtray. His next remark verified this.

'If you need help any time I want you to promise to contact me,' he said evenly.

He looked across the table at her slender, vulnerable sweetness, at the dark brown eyes so attractive against the fair hair, and the sensitive pretty mouth.

A little vexedly he added, 'You shouldn't have come here on your own in the present circumstances. Had you no man friend who might have come with you?' He leaned back in his chair, keeping his eyes upon her face. 'Don't get me wrong. This island is one of the safest places to be in at the moment. I meant...' he made an expressive gesture with a lean brown hand, 'you're a very attractive girl. Need I say more?'

Nora leaned forward to put out her cigarette in the ashtray.

'Nice of you to be so concerned. By the way, I don't usually allow men to pick me up as you did earlier on,' she said quickly. 'But the circumstances were exceptional. I wanted to get out of my wet things as quickly as possible.' She eyed him for a second beneath her lashes. 'I...I never expected to...be brought on this boat.'

His smile was cynical. 'You mean you suspected I had ulterior motives? I'm not blaming you, it shows you aren't just a pretty face. But while we're on the subject I don't usually have to kidnap the girls I fancy. They always come willingly enough.'

Nora lifted her glance again to his briefly, and felt the colour rush to her face. She had no idea why she should feel so tense, unless it was a kind of a sense of loss culminating into a pain at his subtle admission that he did not want her on his boat particularly.

Her throat was dry. She said offhandedly, 'I'm very grateful for your hospitality.'

'No trouble.'

That careless nonchalance was back again in full force, Nora thought—if he had ever lost it. His frank open way of looking her in the eye, his humorous expression from time to time lifting the corners of his well-cut mouth, all added to any physical attractions he possessed, and these were considerable. It was easy to believe that the girls came running, and just as easy to imagine them getting their come-uppance. As far as Nora was concerned he certainly brightened the landscape. It occurred to her in that moment that the light coming through the windows lighting up the interior of the boat was not so bright.

'More coffee?' he asked.

'No, thanks. You did say you were putting my wet things to dry on the deck?'

'That's right.'

He had risen to his feet after putting the cups and plates they had used on the tray.

'Well, I ... I don't suppose they'll be dry for a long time. That is if the sun isn't out.'

'Right again,' he answered laconically, surveying her with a look she could not read.

She waited until it became obvious that he was not going to help her out, although he must have known what she was getting at.

'That being so ... er ...' she floundered on, 'I think I'd better make my way back to the flat like this. No one will notice me particularly. I've noticed that Ramsey isn't overrun with visitors to the pier or the beach in this particular corner.'

He raised a dark brow and picked up the tray. 'If that's what you want. You could stay for lunch if you want—you're welcome to. Please yourself.'

Nora rose to her feet to follow him into the galley. 'I think it's best. My clothes really want the sea water washing out of them. You don't mind me going in your clothes? I'll return them to you.'

'If that's what you want I'll take you ashore in the dinghy. I can land you right opposite to your flat.'

She laughed, a sweet husky sound, and he raised a provocative brow as she regarded him curiously.

'Why didn't you take me ashore in the first place

instead of bringing me to the boat?' she asked frankly.

His firm mouth curved upwards endearingly and her heart played tricks. He was having a strange effect upon her. Steady now! she told herself. The man is a born charmer. He can also tie you into knots.

He said coolly, 'I wanted you to get out of those wet things quickly. Besides, how was I to know you would make yourself a warm drink left on your own?'

For some reason Nora felt wildly happy. 'You're going to make some girl a wonderful husband one day.'

He shook his head with a devilish grin. 'I know when I'm lucky. I'd hate to kiss the same face at breakfast every morning. Sure you won't change your mind about dining with me this evening?'

Nora shook her head, but he asked her again as he helped her from the boat after taking her ashore.

'No, thanks. Where shall I send your clothes?'

He handed her the plastic bag containing her wet things and took his time looking at her windblown hair and her dainty figure swallowed up in his sweater and slacks. Then he said slowly,

'Keep them until I collect them, although I'm not sure I want them back. They'll enjoy hugging you much better.'

That evening, washing out her clothes, Nora knew why she had refused Juan Cregeen's invitation out that night, knew why she had refused him when she wanted to accept. There was no way of putting into words exactly why she had to run away and go on running from a disturbing presence that had affected her like no other had ever done.

She was in danger of falling in love for the first time in her life. Not that she had never been in love. But this was different. And there was nothing worse than falling in love with a man who had openly confessed to her that he had no intention of marrying ever. Even so, Nora had the feeling that she would never run fast enough or far enough to get away from him, and there was not a thing she could do about it. Running away from Juan Cregeen would make no difference at all to her feelings for him.

She washed her sea-soaked clothes, then washed her hair and had a bath. As she towelled herself dry misery tore a jagged edge through her emotions. The feeling was all too familiar since losing her parents, a kind of self-pity. It was a state of mind she had to shake herself out of.

Lying in bed, accommodating her slight figure to the comfort of fresh silky sheets and the soft caress of her gossamer nightdress on her limbs, Nora tried to empty her mind of the day's happenings. Pushing back her hair, baby-soft from washing, she closed her eyes until the soft wash of the tide outside her window lulled her to sleep.

CHAPTER TWO

NORA had strolled out for the morning newspaper and was surprised to find a small packet on the floor of the tiny hall on her return. Someone had obviously dropped it through her letter box while she had been out.

Inside were the keys to a car which was in garage number three on the ground floor below the flats. There was a note enclosed by her lawyer along with the keys, explaining that the new car went with the flat and was the personal bequest of Jed Kelly. It was hers without reservations.

Nora had her breakfast and prepared to go out. Unlocking the garage, she found herself gazing at a gleaming cream Morris car with seat upholstered in primrose.

The car was cheerful, it was merry, and Nora viewed it with delight. She liked the standard radio, the tinted glass, the fog lights, and the alloy wheels. The interior was just as pleasing, with plenty of stowage place and a carpet-lined spacious trunk.

'Very nice!'

She swung round to see Juan Cregeen strolling towards her. She was aware of his glance sliding over her slim shoulders, trim waist and long legs in green slacks. Then the dark eyes were on her face, mocking her rising colour as they studied the cut of her delicate nose before lingering on her pink lips.

There was a young untouched look about her stressed by the crisp cotton top she wore. He liked the proud tilt to her chin, the way her brows arched

32

and straightened upwards emphasising the high cheekbones.

'Glad you like it,' she answered pointedly.

'Who wouldn't?' His grin was unabashed. 'I like the chassis.'

The soft colour sped under her clear skin and she lowered her lashes.

'A present from my benefactor,' she said coolly, feeling anything but. 'I suppose you've come for your clothes. I have them ready.'

He stuck his hands in his pockets. 'Do I look the kind of guy who's short of a sweater and pants?' His mouth twisted in a sardonic smile. 'Go easy on the roads, won't you, we have quite a few blind corners on the island.'

She said frankly, 'That's what I'm afraid of. I'd like to have someone with me for an outing or two, until I get the feel of the road.'

He shrugged. 'You'll soon get into it, since you'll practically be going over the same road many times. You can't go wrong if you read the signs. Done much driving?'

'Oh yes. I can find my way about everywhere in England. But this is a strange island.'

'Don't look so nervous,' he teased, 'or I'm going to hate meeting you on the highway.'

Nora was silent for a few moments, the sunlight on her face. Then she said, 'I don't suppose you'd care to come out with me for a trial run?'

His keen eyes flashed over her face before looking the car over.

'If that's what you want,' he answered. 'You want to go now, right away?'

'Yes, please,' was Nora's instant and enthusiastic reply.

He grinned at her and opened the door of the car. 'Hop in,' he invited.

She paused and gazed at him. 'You mean I'm going to drive?'

'That is the intention. You're going to be fine.'

Nora set the car moving easily, backing out of the garage and waiting while Juan closed the garage door.

'Turn right,' he ordered as he slipped into the seat beside her.

'You mean take the coast road to Douglas?'

'That's right. We can go as far as Laxey and come back on the mountain road.'

Juan settled himself back in his seat comfortably. 'Quite a car. Take it nice and gentle on the corners, won't you? I'd use second gear for a while until you get the feel of them.'

Nora found the car responding to her touch in a way that gave her confidence. As they climbed upwards out of Ramsey she began to enjoy it.

She said after a while, 'I hope I'm not taking you away from something important. It's very kind of you to come with me.'

He said easily. 'There's nothing that can't wait.' He turned sideways to look at her profile. 'Tell me, why didn't you ask Jony to take you around?'

'He's a farmer, isn't he? Besides, he isn't as easy to talk to as you,' she replied, keeping her eyes on the road. 'I don't think he has much to do with women.'

He laughed at this, a deep masculine laugh, and she turned her head to see the flash of white teeth in his tanned face.

'What's so funny?' she cried indignantly.

'That is. Jony has had a girl for the last ten years.' His mouth twisted in a sardonic smile. 'Everybody stopped asking him when he's going to marry ages ago.'

Nora said firmly, 'If a man expected me to wait

that long I'm afraid I'd be gone well before we reached the ten-year mark. What about you?'

Juan laughed. 'I'm easy. I enjoy my life, which is more than can be said for lots of people.'

'Don't you want to settle down?'

'Never had the urge to. I'd have to meet someone I could feel a real hunger for.'

'Don't you believe in love?' she asked.

'Do you?'

'Every girl does. And I don't like cynics. They're usually more romantic than the rest of us.'

He said lazily, 'You mean this love at first sight stuff?'

He was teasing her and she knew it, so it was up to her whether or not she fell for it.

'It has happened,' she shrugged.

'If you go looking for it.'

His voice was so mocking that she cast him an indignant glance.

'You know,' she said with spirit, 'I'm beginning to think I misjudged Jony. At least, he's human!'

'Steady on now,' he warned. 'This is a nasty corner. Take it easy.'

Nora took the corner beautifully. 'You needn't be scared,' she said with dignity. 'I've been well trained in the U.K. in all the congested areas.'

He smiled. 'I'm not criticising your driving. I only think it's most important to look where you're going.'

'I usually do when I'm driving,' she answered sweetly. 'I take it that your last remark relates to other things like getting married? Like most men, you fight shy of it.'

'We Celts are a cautious race. You don't have to know a girl to want her. There's a kind of rapport between you at first meeting. Your eyes collide and are fused together in a kind of electric shock. To anyone like you this is what you've been looking for. You recognise it as being the real thing, a kind of conviction that you're just right for each other when that might not be the case at all.'

Nora coloured up to the soft fair hair clustering around her blue-veined temples.

'Goodness, you are a cynic, aren't you?' she said on an odd little note.

'Why?' he challenged unabashed. 'Because having looked into someone's eyes in passing I then continue on my way? I've lived to tell the tale.'

'What tale? There's none to tell, is there? You didn't even kiss and run,' she cried scornfully.

'Should I have done? It's an idea.'

He reacted to the stiffness in her tone. She knew he was watching her intently, but there was nothing alarming in his scrutiny. He spoke with absolute gentleness.

'I shouldn't advise you to do that. Most men are good at running after someone who takes their fancy.'

And you've taken mine, she thought, seeing without looking the wide forehead, hair squared at the temples balanced by a firm determined jawline, nose slightly beaked with sensitive nostrils and a mobile mouth which was in the habit of lifting at the corners. All this with the square-shouldered vigour of muscled arms had floored her as no man had.

She said, 'Do you work for a living or do you just laze around?'

'I work. Something to do with boats,' Juan answered laconically. 'What do you do?'

'I'm an estate agent, among other things.'

He laughed softly. 'A career girl? Any good at it?'

'I have a partner, and we're doing fine, thank you.'

'Congratulations!'

She shot him a swift glance. 'You sound disappointed?'

'Surprised is more like it.' He looked lazily over her slim figure. 'You don't look like a career girl for a start. Certainly not one of the clever ones.'

'I didn't say I was clever.'

'You can't be dumb if you're making the business pay. Who's your partner? Another woman?' he asked sardonically.

'No, a man.'

'Good.' Juan was leaning forward examining the gadgets in front of him before turning his intelligent gaze around the interior of the car.

Instantly piqued, Nora cried, 'What do you mean by that?'

'By what?' His gaze came back to her. 'You mean working with a man? Make you more human.'

'Really? You approve of that, do you?' Nora smiled, her composure completely restored. 'What have you got against girls having a career?'

'Easy now. Blind corner ahead,' he warned as her eyes met his.

Nora took it a little wide on a screech of brakes and he cringed theatrically.

'Sorry,' she said sweetly. 'I hope I haven't scared you.'

'You probably scared the car,' he grinned. 'How's it going?'

'Like a dream. Want to try it?'

'After our stop at Laxey.'

Laxey nestled in the foothills, a secluded little bay way down below the coast road. Nora stopped the car at Juan's request by a picturesque inn at the entrance to beautiful gardens.

'We'll go down to the beach another day,' he said, leading her to a gay canopied table for two near the door of the inn. The other tables were occupied by holidaymakers and Nora gazed about her with shining eyes.

'Nice,' she commented. 'Do you come here often?'

'Inside,' he said with a grin.

Nora gazed around her with delight at the beautiful trees leading to the gardens, presenting him with the smooth creamy curve of her cheek and the enchanting sweep of dark lashes. Sensing his eyes upon her, she turned instinctively as he captured her gaze.

'Cigarette?' he asked as she finished her drink.

She shook her head, like spun gold in the rays of the sun, and her heart missed a beat from the sudden gladness which swept over her. Suddenly she knew she liked Juan, and wanted to be friends with him. It was not just physical attraction. There was something about him—a charm entirely his own. He was the kind of man who would be completely indifferent to what anyone thought about him, and yet there was a touch of arrogance about his lack of self-consciousness.

Juan finished lighting the cigarette which he had put between his lips and, snapping shut his lighter, leaned back in his chair and pushed the skipper's hat he wore to the back of rough dark curls. The cream polo-necked sweater topped navy corduroys and his long legs tapered into sneakers.

'Not a bad spot, is it?' he said.

She laughed. 'It's beautiful.' A frown flitted across her smooth forehead. 'Have you been courting for ten years too?' she asked thoughtfully.

He laughed. 'No, I haven't. Disappointed?'

'I don't know. I'd have to think about it. The thing is that Jony has, and therefore he won't be interested in marrying me for a further share of Mr Kelly's estate.'

Juan blew a line of cigarette smoke thoughtfully into the air.

'I wouldn't bank on that if I were you. He has a lot to gain by getting his hands on the lot. Land is fetching an enormous price now and speculators are queueing up for it.'

'You mean to say that the man would be mean enough to ditch the girl he's been going out with for ten years for a bit of extra money?' she burst out.

'It has happened.' A pause. 'Would you be interested in settling on the island?'

'I've never given it a thought.' Nora looked up to meet his eyes. 'I'd never marry just to conform to the terms of a will.'

'Marry a Manxman, you mean?' he said lazily.

'That's right.'

'But you haven't met many, have you? I can introduce you to quite a few nice ones.' He grinned as he tapped ash from his cigarette. 'One or two of them are mad on boats. Do you like sailing?'

'I haven't done any.' She would like to bet that he was one of the 'mad on boats' kind. His strong brown hands looked suited to grasping ropes and hauling in sails and those wide, powerful shoulders had developed through wrestling against the elements while afloat. His steady intelligent eyes implied honesty, but it was his sense of humour that revealed more of his personality. She was interested, too interested in him to let their friendship go any further. Yet she could not help herself.

'Too much of a challenge, is it?' he queried, amused at her wary expression. 'No one will rush you into marriage although I dare say some will be interested in the bait.'

Her cheeks coloured. 'That's a crude way of putting it!' she cried resentfully. 'I suppose it's living by the sea that accounts for you being so down-to-earth in your attitude.'

'We're certainly nearer to nature than you city dwellers,' he said reasonably, and consulted his watch. 'We'd better move. We can go back along the mountain road and I'll drive if you like.'

He pointed out superb views as they sped on with only a few sheep for company on the hills. Several cars were parked by peat beds and whole families were carrying wads of it to their car trunk.

'Nice car. Goes like a dream,' he said. 'If you land a husband as tractable you'll be a very lucky girl.'

'I don't think that's funny,' Nora retorted. 'Besides, who wants a mouse instead of a man?'

He lifted a dark brow provocatively and tossed her an approving glance.

'Exactly my sentiments. Like to take the wheel?'

'No,' she said hastily, meeting a quizzical glance. She was enjoying seeing him behind the wheel, and his presence was very comforting. It was easy to imagine any girl becoming interested in him. 'Wonderful views from up here,' she added.

He said casually, 'You see them all the year round in the colours of all the seasons. Lucky today that there isn't a mist, so your views are panoramic.'

'I never knew there was so much of the countryside untouched.' She smiled at the beautiful pattern of browns, greens and yellows of fields stretching for miles among the glens. The road along which they travelled was without the shelter of hedges and with few houses to be seen there was an almost primitive look about it.

They were going down into Ramsey when Juan asked, 'What about going out with me this evening? We can take this car and you can discover the hazards of driving at night.'

Nora looked at him quickly, and the clear flicker of suspicion on her face was there for him to see. After all, what did she know about him? Not as much as she knew about Jony, even! And to go out with him that evening driving in the dark with only open country for miles around was simply asking for trouble.

His voice was rough at the edges. 'Don't you trust me? I don't eat little girls for supper.'

Her eyes fell away from his. 'I'm sorry,' she answered. 'I usually get more notice than a few hours for a date. I hate to be rushed into anything.'

'Really? You rushed into trying out the car willingly enough this morning. Anyway, I'll give you the benefit of the doubt. Forget I asked you.'

Nora began to feel ashamed of herself. At the moment his eyes were on the road ahead and she glanced at him surreptitiously beneath her eyelashes. There was an assurance about him which belied anything small and mean, and he seemed to have an abundance of common sense. Why then was she dithering about going out with him?

She said impulsively, 'What had you planned for this evening? Dining somewhere a car distance away?'

'Forget it,' he answered in icy tones.

'I can't. I didn't mean to hurt your feelings, but you must see that ... well, lots of things have been happening since I came here, and ...'

'And you can't be too careful? Is that what you're trying to say?' he finished for her.

'In a way,' she replied in tones just as icy. 'I am here on holiday in a way, but that doesn't mean I'm out for cheap thrills.'

'All right, you've made your point.' He spoke brusquely as if there was nothing more to be said, and Nora sank back in her seat feeling somewhat deflated. She had thrown his friendship back in his face. It was not the way she would have chosen to state her case, but Juan Cregeen had to know she was not the kind of girl to be taken lightly. There must have been many he had taken in that vein, since he was by far too attractive to women.

They were now coming into Ramsey and he made short work of the distance to her flat. Sitting in the car while he opened the garage door, Nora attempted to put a good face on it as she climbed from her seat before leaving the car. But her tense unhappy expression persisted.

She walked out of the garage while Juan set about closing the door after her. Then giving her the car keys, he said roughly,

'Got a problem, haven't you? You'll never be sure whether or not any future proposals you might have will be given with your inheritance in mind?'

Her small laugh fell flat. 'That's flattering, I must say!'

'It's the truth.' he said bluntly.

'I suppose it is, providing I accept the conditions of the will. Well, thanks for the outing. It had its moments.'

Her fingers brushed his as they closed over the keys and she tensed against the impact, wondering what chemistry it was that made one person affect the senses above all others.

Back in her flat Nora strolled to the window to gaze out over the sea. The old frightened feeling of being alone came over her. It was the same now wherever she went. Juan had brought it all back— the feeling of belonging to someone, of being cosseted by a loved one.

Juan was the type of man who would look after someone rather than expect them to look after him. She had been wise to refuse to go out with him. It had not been him that she could not trust, it was herself.

But taking a shower that evening while making up her mind whether to eat out or not after refusing to go out with Juan did not seem so smart after all. Without being aware of it Nora dressed as if for a date.

Should she decide to eat out there was nothing to prevent her going through the communicating door leading into the restaurant adjoining the flats. The sudden peal of her doorbell startled her and she went forward to open it on a subtle wave of perfume.

'Juan!' she exclaimed, with the feeling of having been running. 'Of course, you've come for your clothes. I'm sorry, I ought to have given them to you this afternoon.'

He laughed. 'I suppose that's as good an excuse as any for calling.'

'You are the most unpredictable man!' she burst out.

'For what? For thinking you really hadn't anywhere special to go this evening?'

Her cheeks flamed. 'How do you know I haven't?' she cried indignantly. 'I'm not exactly dressed for staying in.'

His eyes roved over the slender figure in swirling chiffon, taking in the darkness of her eyes against the fairness of her hair. His reaction to her youthful freshness was a faint narrowing of his eyes.

He said pleasantly, 'Nice to see you're ready to go out. I was considering telephoning you but decided at the last moment to collect you.' Then, as if in afterthought, he added, 'Seeing that you're anxious to settle your mind about driving on the island, tonight is as good as any to help you to become accustomed to driving in the dark.'

'But it isn't dark. It won't be for hours yet.'

'True, but by the time we come back it will be. Plenty of cloud tonight, so there won't be a moon.'

Nora wished he would not look at her so intently. It was distinctly unnerving. Suspicion became a tight feeling in her stomach and she tried to hide it by flippancy.

'You're being much too kind. I couldn't take advantage of you again after this morning.'

'I haven't changed my plans for this evening to suit you.' He eyed her with the cool, aloof interest as a doctor would a patient. 'Now you have the car you might as well get used to it and make the most of the time you're here. You can drive anywhere on the island and feel safe from attacks, and the roads are good and well marked. Just take care not to speed on awkward bends, that's all.'

Nora was past speech. She saw the haughty outline of his head against the lights behind him in the corridor, the indolent posture as he leaned against the door frame with wide, immaculately clad shoulders, and felt a sudden challenge to know more about him.

'Got your car keys?' Juan's deep voice prodded her into speech.

'They're in my purse.'

Turning round from him, Nora swiftly went back into the lounge to pick up her purse and to snatch a stole from a closet.

'I'm dining with friends,' he said as they made their way along the corridor to the lift. 'They're quite used to me bringing someone with me, so you'll be very welcome.'

Nora did not lift her head but kept her eyes on the carpet as they entered the lift.

So she was to be another of his girl friends. Who was she following, the beautiful dark-haired Tricia whom he had been towing across the water?

'Where are we making for?' she asked as the lift doors opened on the ground floor.

'In the country.'

Her head jerked up then. 'I see what you mean it being dark later on. There won't be any lights at all for miles, will there, when we come back?'

'That's right. You'll meet very few cars, so you'll be broken in gently to night driving.' He let this sink in, then, 'I'll drive going and you can look for landmarks as we go, because I'm leaving you to bring us back.'

Slipping into the driving seat beside her, he waited for her to fasten her seat belt, then fastened his own, and in a moment the car was moving.

'You're very quiet,' he commented.

They had left the coast behind and were making for the open country.

'Perhaps I'm looking for those landmarks.'

He said casually, 'The main roads are easy to follow. It's the turnings of the country lanes that you have to remember.' He laughed on recognising the look she shot at him. 'You're worried, aren't you? I'm trying to figure out whether you are worried about driving in the dark or about me.'

Her answer came swiftly, 'I am in the dark about you, so it isn't the darkness of the country roads on our return journey which worries me.' Her eyes were sparks of anger. 'I just have to trust you.'

'You can,' laconically.

'Good. Then perhaps we can get on to a less boring subject.'

Raising a dark sardonic brow, he shot her a whimsical glance.

'I can always hot the conversation up, make it more exciting, if that's what you want?'

Nora said hastily, 'I'll manage, thanks.'

And that, she told herself, was what she had to do. The island was having an unsettling effect upon her, including Juan. But it was not Juan entirely. There was the condition in her benefactor's will, the fact that a great deal of money was involved and that he wanted her to have a share of it. Nora knew that normally she would have accepted what was hers and come to some arrangement with Jony about the money and income involved. But she did not want to let Mr Kelly down by not carrying out his wishes. There were lots of things she could do with the money if she did not want it for herself.

Their destination was a farmhouse set in the country and backed by hills. Built of Manx stone, it was sturdy and had remained untouched through the years.

'What an enchanting place,' Nora murmured as he swung the car up the tree-lined narrow lane leading to it.

'Belongs to a friend of mine. He has guests staying with him at the moment,' Juan explained. 'You've already seen one of them at a distance.'

'Tricia?' she said, and felt an unease which was unexplainable.

'The very same.'

He swung the car to a halt behind several others on the drive, and helped her out.

A tall blond man stood waiting to greet them at the door. The slight thickening of his waist suggested that he was around forty.

'Good evening, Juan. Glad you could make it.' His wide grin included them both, but his blue eyes rested curiously on Nora.

Juan said easily, 'Nora, Finn Cullan. Finn, Nora Bain, on holiday here.'

Nora liked the firm grip of the hand that closed on hers. His look of appraisal was within the bounds of courtesy and the superb cut of his grey business suit was matched by his manner.

A door to their left in the hall was open and voices came from the room on light waves of laughter. Among a dozen or so guests a young woman was holding court. The red bathing suit which had adorned her shapely figure was gone and in its place was a rather low-cut gown in green that emphasised the green of her eyes. Her dark hair with auburn overtones was parted in the middle with soft waves of hair detracting considerably from the hardness of her features.

Tricia, thought Nora, as the girl came forward to give her a rapier-like glance before smiling angelically at Juan. She held Juan's arm as he introduced them for all the world as if she had a prior claim on him.

Nora watched him, saw his easy smile as he took in the plunging neckline and provocative smile.

'So glad you're here, darling,' Tricia was smiling up into his eyes. 'Aimée wants to see you before she goes to sleep. I'll take care of Nora.'

As Juan hesitated, Nora felt herself tightening up inside without knowing why she should. But she did wonder who Aimée might be.

'Aimée is my daughter,' Tricia explained. 'The poor darling is just recovering from an attack of polio. She's very fond of Juan—he's been so kind to her.' She sighed theatrically. 'He knows what a burden she is to me and takes her out to give me a break.'

Nora said, 'I'm sorry. I saw you in the bay the other evening, didn't I?'

Another exaggerated sigh. 'I'm afraid I'm very protective where Aimée is concerned. She's only ten years old—I married very young. You have no idea what it means meeting someone as understanding as Juan.'

I can guess, Nora thought wryly. Her throat was behaving oddly and it was necessary to keep on swallowing to ease the dryness. The woman was shallow, she sensed it. All her mannerisms were too theatrical to be genuine and Nora could not for the life of her see Tricia in the role of ministering angel to her daughter. Poor little mite! It was to Juan's credit that he was showing compassion for the child, but she wondered how far he would be taken in by the mother.

Tricia evidently believed in putting all her goods on display, like going surf-riding with Juan. What better way to show off her feminine charms than in a brief swimsuit? Furthermore, she was nearer Juan's age, although she did not look it.

'Where did you and Juan meet?' she asked.

Shaken out of her reverie by the question, Nora sensed the antagonism in Tricia's voice.

Airily she said, 'On the pier at Ramsey.'

The green eyes glanced calculatingly at Nora's ringless hands.

'You're not engaged or married?' she asked curiously.

'Should I be?'

Tricia had the grace to blush. 'I was only wondering why Juan brought you with him. He probably thought there would be some young men here for you to meet.'

'You know, you could be right,' Nora remarked with a smile on her lips. 'I like Juan. He has a congenital charm, he's very intelligent and very commanding. His charm works whether he's lazy and watchful or vital and domineering.'

Tricia looked a bit taken aback and Nora found she was enjoying herself.

'Oh ... er ... yes. Do come and meet everybody,' she invited weakly.

Most of the guests were young, but everyone seemed to be paired off. Nora accepted a drink and talked for some time with a young couple who ran an arts and craft shop on the island.

Then Juan was there, and her heart missed a beat as he scanned the room in search of her. He was with his host, against whose lightness of colouring he seemed even darker and taller—saturnine in a subdued way.

Nora felt emotions working up inside her as she met his white smile across the room. Come, come, this won't do, she told herself. You'll meet scores of attractive men before you go back home.

The evening passed pleasantly with more guests drifting in later. Everyone drifted into the big beautifully fitted kitchen to help themselves from mounds of all kinds of food from caviare to cheese biscuits.

Nora filled her plate sparingly and sat on a window seat with Juan in the lounge to enjoy it. Juan grinned down at her as she ate daintily. Her clear skin had a pale gold look overlaid by a pink bloom. Her eyes, clear and bright, were veiled by a thick fringe of lashes. Her silky hair had a pure golden sheen and her lips curved into an impish smile.

His mocking smile teased. 'Enjoying yourself?' he asked. 'Glad you came?'

She nodded and popped a tiny vol-au-vent of prawns into her mouth.

'Who's Finn Cullan? He evidently has plenty of money,' she asked curiously.

'A millionaire sportsman. He has a yacht in the bay at Port St Mary. Lost his wife two years ago.'

'And Tricia?'

'Finn met her at a yacht club in the south of

England, found out about her daughter and invited them here for a spell.' He laughed at the expression on her face. 'There's no chance of Finn marrying again, least of all Tricia. That was what you were thinking, wasn't it?'

Sharply, she said, 'No, I wasn't. I didn't know whether Tricia already has a husband.'

'She hasn't. If she ever had one.'

Nora's eyes widened in surprise. 'You mean she might never have been married?'

'That's right.'

'Then I suppose she's to be admired for keeping the child instead of sending it to a home.'

He nodded in agreement. 'Aimée is quite a handful, poor sweet.'

Nora said slowly, 'I could help Aimée and others like her if I had my share of the legacy with Jony.'

'True, but I would decide against it. I would also let Jony know you would never entertain the idea of marrying a Manxman in order to inherit.'

'You'd like me to tell Jony I wouldn't even consider marrying him if he asked me or something to that effect? I don't think he would ask me.'   .

'I wouldn't be too sure. I told you what land is fetching, and Jony is only human where money is concerned.'

'Even so, I might not want to lose his friendship,' she said perversely.

'Have you forgotten he has a girl-friend?' Juan's look of appraisal had a sharpness in its tail. 'Don't tell me his Marlon Brando scowl has you hooked.' Narrow-eyed with lips that had gone tight, he went on, 'He's not only the biggest bore for miles, he's mean with it.'

'And I suppose he drinks heavily,' she added sarcastically.

'When someone else pays for it. You ought to

meet his girl-friend—she's far too good for him.'

Nora said gently, 'She must love him a lot.'

He said harshly, 'Pity he didn't marry her years ago. That would have cured her.'

'No, it wouldn't. Not if she truly loves him.'

He chuckled. 'You have a lot to learn! Fate is just straining on her leash to have a go at you. I'm going to get you a cup of coffee. No more wine—you're driving us back.'

While he went for coffee, Nora looked at the other guests draped around the room. Finn Cullan was moving in between them smiling and talking with charm. Nora wondered what his wife had been like and realised that he filled his need of her company by the parties he gave. She saw Tricia approach him, but his reaction to her provocative look was to pat her bare shoulder in a fatherly way and move on.

Nora went cold at the thought of the girl turning her charms upon Juan. Would he eventually succumb? It was on the cards that had she not come with him this evening he would certainly have come to see Tricia.

He was back with the coffee. 'Here you are. Yours is white and sweet—just like you. Mine is black, so beware.'

They left at eleven o'clock. Juan said, 'Can't have you going to sleep behind the wheel, can we?'

He saw her behind the wheel of the car, then slid in beside her. Nora started the car and slowly moved it down the driveway of trees. It was almost dark as she joined the main road. There was no moon and the roads were unlit as they sped between sentinels of trees.

To her chagrin Juan leaned back in his seat and closed his eyes with the intention of leaving her to it. Nora's fingers tightened on the wheel. She would show him! She had pinpointed the turnings they had taken in coming, and although the roads looked very different in the dark her confidence was good.

There were few cars on the road and they dipped their headlights politely so there was no threat of glare. If it had not been essential for Nora to keep her attention fixed on the roads ahead, she would have enjoyed it. To find herself alone with a very attractive and charming man was in itself a pleasure.

'You're staring too hard. Blink a few times and relax. Silly to tire your eyes—that way you can easily drop asleep without knowing it.'

The deep voice penetrated the silence and Nora flung him a look which cut him down to size.

'Thanks for the tip,' she retorted through clenched teeth. 'The motoring association must be crying out for instructors like you. Just leave me alone! Only when you do fall asleep take care you don't topple from that high pedestal you're sitting on.'

'Thrown off is more appropriate, wouldn't you say?' he murmured. 'You will observe that I have my seat belt fastened.'

'I'd like to put it around your neck and pull it hard,' she blurted. 'You are the most exasperating man!'

'Calm down, and remember you're driving by signposts. It's so easy to take the wrong road in the dark.'

They flashed by a side road which Nora hardly noticed in her anger. Juan was mocking her in the way that most men mocked women drivers.

'Thanks again,' she said sarcastically. 'I'll restrain myself from running into the nearest tree.'

There was no more conversation and the muted hum of the engine was the only sound. The car was eating up miles and miles of country road with only an occasional cottage or farmhouse lighted up by the headlights on the way. Then gradually it occurred to Nora that the signposts she slowed down to look at had unfamiliar names.

She bit hard on her lip. Juan had not opened his eyes and she was determined not to rouse him to ask his help. It did not help to see truant patches of mist waving in the car's headlights like thick nylon scarves directly in front of her.

Then presently she saw another signpost looming ahead and slowed down again to peer at it. Turning down the car window, she breathed in the cold air. It was then that the police car drew up beside her, and a very nice young man said politely,

'Can I help you, madam?'

Hoping with all her heart that Juan was asleep, Nora said eagerly, 'Yes, you can, officer. I seem to have missed the road to Ramsey.'

'Indeed you have, madam,' he answered crisply. 'But only by a short margin. If you'll turn the car round and follow me I'll take you back to the right road.'

After a swift glance at the silent Juan Nora did as she was told and in five minutes she was on the main road leading directly to Ramsey.

Only when they had reached her flat and the engine was shut off did Juan stir himself.

'Congratulations,' he said. 'You made it.'

'With no thanks to you,' she snapped. 'Well, aren't you going to open the garage door?'

He looked at her disapprovingly. On raised eyebrows he exclaimed, 'Do I detect impatient undertones directed at myself? No one orders me about. Now ask me nicely.'

Nora stared at his changing expression and took fresh umbrage. The tension that had built up in-

side her during the journey was now fit to burst.
Furthermore, it rankled to know that she had had
to be rescued by a police officer, even if he was a
nice one. Now it seemed Juan was intent on humili-
ating her still further. And it was all his fault! He
could easily have put her on the right road. Come
to think of it, he had deliberately needled her into
conversation at the vital moment when she had
overrun the turning into the main road to Ramsey.
He had done it deliberately, of course.

'Men!' she muttered under her breath, and made
to open her door.

Instantly his hand shot out to grip her wrist, and
her look of disgust turned to one of sheer amaze-
ment.

He said coldly, 'I repeat—ask me nicely.'

Nora struggled to free her wrist, to no avail. His
grip was unshakeable no matter how she twisted
and turned her wrist.

'You're hurting me, you big brute!' she cried.
'How dare you manhandle me? Let me go at once!'

'You're hurting yourself by twisting your wrist.
I'll let you go when you've done what I ask.'

Her eyes, brown daggers, clashed with the merciless glint in his.

'I'll never ask anything more of you while I'm
on the island,' she told him furiously. 'Not if we
sit here all night.'

'That's all right with me,' he told her coolly. 'I'm
quite comfortable.'

Nora looked down at the strong brown fingers
curled around her wrist and tears bit in her eyes
at her own helplessness. She hated him, the big
overbearing brute! Fate seemed to be on his side
too, for he had been asleep for the most part during
the car run, while she was tired out by now.

Frustrated minutes ticked by and Nora thought longingly of her bed. She knew when she was beaten. It was one thing to sit beside Juan wide awake in a sleeping world, but quite another to fall asleep and be at his mercy.

Her voice was a mere whisper. 'Would you mind opening the garage door . . . sir?'

The emphasis on the last word was said insultingly, but Juan did not turn a hair.

'Certainly, madam. It's a pleasure.'

He unfolded his long length from the car and to Nora his answer was the last straw. He had imitated the policeman's voice to perfection, thereby revealing the fact that he had been awake at the time of her encounter with the officer of the law.

Words failed her as she drove into the garage. With a set face she waited for him to lock the garage door before putting her hand out for the keys. To her surprise he did no such thing. Instead he took hold of her elbow and began to move along with her to the entrance to the flats.

With her voice on ice, Nora spoke. 'I can find my own way, thanks.'

'All the same, I'll come up with you to your door,' was his answer.

She made no demur since it occurred to her that she could hand over to him the clothes she had borrowed after her fall from the pier. That way she would be rid of him and under no further obligation.

He unlocked the door of her flat, then handed her the keys.

'I'll get your clothes,' she said, and hurried inside.

He stood politely at the door and was leaning negligently against the door frame when she returned.

'Thanks,' he said politely as she thrust the parcel

at him. 'I'd like to congratulate you on your driving this evening. Apart from missing the turning, you did very well.'

His mouth twitched and Nora longed to slam the door in his face, only he happened to be standing deliberately in the way.

She lifted a militant chin. Her eyes were brown sparks of anger. 'Very funny!' she cried in disgust. 'You wanted me to miss that turning!'

He raised a mocking brow. 'Hey now, don't be like that! I did what you wanted by supplying the company to give you the confidence you needed, so what are you so het up about?'

'So het up?' Nora echoed. Words failed her. 'Why, you ... you didn't help me at all!'

He said reasonably, 'But surely that was the point of the whole exercise? I left you on your own for you to react in the way you would to any problems. It was a true test, and you came through it very well.'

But Nora was in no fit state to reason. Her nerves were too raw after an evening which she could not say with truth that she had enjoyed. She felt choked and in need of her bed.

'Look, I'm tired,' she said huskily. 'Goodnight.'

Juan made no move to go. He swung the parcel on a negligent finger and narrowed keen eyes that probed.

'I'm not going until you tell me what's upsetting you,' he told her in steely tones. 'Come on, let's have it.'

But Nora stood her ground, staring at him with animosity and disgust.

Patiently, he went on, 'Look, I know you're tired and that you hated being rescued by the law, but it's something more than that, isn't it? Something against me personally?'

She spoke in the manner of someone being tolerant against their will.

'Can you deny that you weren't asleep when that police car drew up?' she demanded.

'I never said I was, did I?'

Nora drew in a breath that hurt, and went on painfully,

'Do you also deny that you knew I was driving past the turning that would have taken us to Ramsey?'

He said roughly, 'I don't deny anything. You had to find out your own mistakes. When you're driving alone you have to make your own way back to where you want to go. There's a road map in one of the compartments in front of you. You'd better study it before making any more long journeys.'

Nora knew that what he said made sense, but instead of placating her it only seemed to add to her fury. At what seemed to be a stretched moment Juan nonchalantly leaning against the door frame seemed set to prevent her from shutting him out.

It was no use, she told herself despairingly. He would have the last word every time—he was that kind of man. Yet he was proving to be a man of integrity who stood no nonsense. Her kind of man really. What then was the matter with her? She had lowered her eyes to the carpet and his finger beneath her chin felt strong yet gentle. His tone was loaded with charm.

'Come on now, where's your sense of humour? I don't suppose you realise that you probably floored that policeman into making him a friend for life. No need to worry when you're driving in the dark in that part of the island. He'll be there to come to your rescue.'

He looked into her face to see what effect his words were having. 'I'm your friend too if you'll have me. I'm a pretty useful man to have around.'

He gave her the slow lazy smile which always added to her discomfiture. She drew away hurriedly, and said lightly,

'I'm on holiday, remember? I'm sure I shan't have any cause to call for masculine help. If I need any I'll let you know.'

He shrugged. 'If that's what you want,' he agreed coolly. 'Let me know and I might consider it.'

'There's always Jony,' Nora reminded him, feeling more composed since moving back from his touch. His presence was unnerving.

'True. But Jony is a farmer.' He paused, smiled wickedly. 'No doubt he'll find time for you.'

She quivered. 'You're making me feel like some rich heiress who could be held for ransom!'

Juan raised a brow. 'You mean like someone abducting you to force you into marriage in order to share your inheritance?' He shook his head. 'You're safe enough and you have nothing to worry about. Mind you, you could do worse than marry a Manxman. After all, their ideas about marriage are sound enough, and not as distorted as people from across.'

She looked up at him, startled by so much plain speaking. Drat the man! He always seemed to be taking her unawares. No use trying to decipher his enigmatic expression, and she was never sure when he was laughing at her.

She tried attack. 'Are you telling me this on your own behalf? That someone will get a prize if they marry you?'

He threw back his head and laughed. 'Lord, no! I've spent most of my time over the water, so I'm as contaminated as the rest of them.'

'I see,' Nora replied, wishing she could think of something to put him effectively in his place. 'Well, thanks, Juan, for all you've done. Maybe if I meet someone who seems to coincide with my requirements I might get in touch with you to ask your approval.'

He hesitated, his glance at her upturned face deep and probing. Then the mocking smile was back.

'You do that,' he advised. 'Better if he knew nothing about your circumstances. That way he won't feel he's being used.'

The rich colour swept under her clear skin. She said icily,

'Charming! Nice to know that I need money to boost my sex appeal.'

He said harshly, 'You know I didn't mean anything of the kind. You're determined to fall out with me, but it's no go. You're tired, so we'll forget all about it.'

Nora drew in a deep breath. 'You're dead right. I am tired, tired of . . . of your superior advice, and . . . and . . . Oh, go away!' she ended, near to tears.

The parcel slid from his finger to the carpet and her heart fell with it as he grabbed her shoulders.

'All right,' he muttered with tight teeth. 'Have it your way. Only before I go here's something to remember me by.'

His mouth closed suffocatingly on her own trembling one and she ran through a whole gamut of emotions with an element of surprise that gave way eventually to outraged anger. This turned into something so wonderful that it defied description. Her body melted against him as arms like iron bands drew her still closer.

It was not unlike falling from a great height when he eventually let her go. She swayed, wondering what had hit her, bemused beyond words. But Juan was not so starry-eyed. He bent to pick up the parcel he had dropped before hauling her into his arms, then gave her a withering look.

'Nice to have met you, Miss Bain. Do me a favour and forget we met. You have a nice little set-up here. There's no reason why you shouldn't have a nice holiday. Goodbye.'

CHAPTER THREE

In the days which followed Nora had to admit that her encounter with Juan Cregeen had shaken her mentally as well as physically. Being alone she tended to brood upon it at first, acknowledging that while it had upset her it had also rammed home to her the danger of becoming too deeply involved with anyone during her stay on the island.

So gradually she began to enjoy herself, going off in the car to explore the island but doing no more driving at night. The image of the mocking Juan sitting beside her was far too vivid yet to dismiss.

Most days, weather permitting, she bathed in the sea, taking care to use a particular corner of the beach away from where the yachts and boats were moored near to the pier. Neither Juan nor Tricia had put in an appearance on the water again and Nora hoped they would not do so while she was around.

She spent some nights on the balcony of her flat, often taking a stroll before bed either along the shore or, if the tide was in, along the pier, along which there were never more than a dozen people enjoying the evening air.

One night when the tide was in, Nora strolled along the pier, passing the few fisherman who after throwing out a hopeful line were now returning home with their catch. The railway line used by the miniature train which ran down the centre of the pier was strewn with empty mussel shells, a reminder of the skill of the seagulls. They used the rail to smash the mussels open for food.

It was one of those quiet balmy evenings with very little wind, and the sea was as smooth as a mill-pond. The pier was almost deserted now as it drew near to closing time, but Nora reckoned on strolling to the far end and back before the gate was closed.

She drew in deeply of the night air and gazed wistfully across the water turning to gold in the dying rays of the setting sun. With her hands thrust into the pockets of her woolly jacket she strolled along, aware of work in progress on the protective rails enclosing the pier.

The workmen had gone home hours ago, leaving a six-foot length of rail still to be put up. A rope had been put across the space and Nora was on her way back along the pier when she noticed the small purse lying on the edge of the space over the water.

At first sight of it her heart lurched. Had someone gone off the pier into the water leaving the purse? She walked to the edge of the space and looked over, but there was no sign of anyone in the water, although the rope had been unhooked leaving the space unprotected. The purse, a plastic one, was empty. It was the kind that a child would have, and she wondered if children had unhooked the rope while playing there, and realising the time, they had gone, hence the purse which one of them might easily have dropped. The sudden thrust between her shoulder blades sent her hurtling through space and the scream from her lips was lost in the cries of seagulls overhead.

After the shock of sudden impact with the water, Nora reared her head and shaking the water from her eyes swam strongly for the shore. The tide was on its way out and was lapping greedily around the girders of the pier. It would have been easier to swim to the iron steps leading up on to the pier, but she had no wish to meet the person who had pushed her into the water in a place that would now be deserted.

Fortunately the tide had receded from the sea wall enough by the time she got there for her to walk along until she was opposite to her flat. But the going had been rough. There had been a formidable stretch of water to plough through, but fear had lent her speed and she surprised herself by her stamina in making it to the shore.

By the time she heaved herself from the water she was shaking with shock and torn between the need to cry or be sick. But she had made it and she was safe. Stumbling along the beach within the shelter of the high sea wall, she finally reached the stone steps leading on to the promenade, and there across the road was her flat.

A boy with his dog stared at her at the top of the steps and a young couple strolling arm in arm did the same as she hurried by on her way to the flat.

Nora was in the entrance hall when she remembered her shoulder bag. It had gone, and she laughed a trifle hysterically to find that she was still clutching the plastic purse. Her keys were in her bag and she could not get into her flat without them.

The porter in charge of the flats eyed her in comical dismay when she found him.

'What did you do?' he queried. 'Drop your bag in the sea and go in after it?'

She gulped and decided to play along with him. 'Silly of me, wasn't it?' with chattering teeth.

'Very,' he said dryly. 'Not to worry, I'll ask a friend of mine to comb the beach later when the tide has gone out. He might find it.'

She thanked him when he had unlocked her door

and he gave her a friendly smile.

'We'll have keys ready for you if your bag isn't found, so don't worry,' he said, and bade her good-night.

Nora could only nod her head because her teeth were chattering too much for her to speak. The warm air of her flat met her like open arms and the hot bath purged away all the cold sense of shock. When she was dry she snuggled into a bathrobe and made a hot drink.

Then came all the questions going around in her head like clothes in a tumble-dryer. With her fingers curled around the hot drink and her legs tucked under her in the chair she asked herself why on earth anyone on a strange island would want to harm her. It did not make sense, unless...could it have been Jony? After all, he was the one who would benefit from the will if anything happened to her.

Nora lay in bed trying to solve the mystery until her eyelids began to droop and sleep claimed her. The peal of her doorbell tore into her unconsciousness with a continued insistence. Whoever it was kept their finger on the bell and was evidently not going away.

Half asleep, she fell out of bed and reached for her wrap, tying it around her as she staggered to the door. The porter could have waited until morning, if it was him to give her news of her shoulder bag. Five o'clock was a bit much to expect her to welcome him with open arms.

But it was not the porter who confronted her, and it was some seconds before her mind began to function. Juan, she thought, looking terribly distraught was pushing back his dark hair with raking fingers.

'Thank God!' he cried. 'Are you all right?'

'Of course I'm all right,' she answered. 'How did you get in? The hall door to the flats is usually locked at night.'

He said impatiently, 'Came in with some late night revellers. Aren't you going to ask me in?'

'At this hour in the morning?'

'I've got this,' he answered, and thrust her shoulder bag at her. 'I can't tell you how I felt when I found it. I've never looked through anything so quick in my life to make sure that it was yours!'

Nora took the bag and stepped back. 'You'd better come in,' she said, and followed him into the lounge. 'Where did you find it, and how did you know I'd lost it?'

'Hell!' he exclaimed, flinging himself into a chair and gesturing with a long brown hand. 'How would I know you'd lost it? The trouble is that up to five minutes ago I thought you were lost with it. What the devil was it doing in the sea?'

Nora stood looking down at him with her fingers coiled around the shoulder bag. Suspicions were running around in her head like a demented hornet. She was suspicious of everyone—Jony, Tricia, even Juan, who knew she could swim and who would see no point in pushing her into the water even if he had wanted to. Besides, he looked upset as if he was suffering from shock.

She hesitated, then said in a small voice, 'Thank you for the bag. I dropped it into the sea as I was diving in from the pier.'

Juan looked startled at that. 'Diving from the pier with your shoulder bag? What would you be doing that for?' A smile that did not reach his eyes lifted the corners of his mouth. 'You didn't happen to want to put an end to it all on account of our falling out?'

'Very funny! No, I was pushed from the pier.'

'Pushed?' he echoed incredulously. 'Who would want to push you off the pier? Was it vandals?'

'I don't think so. I never heard a sound, no voices or anything. It was around quarter to ten and the pier was deserted as far as I could see.'

Instantly he had leapt to his feet to grip her slim shoulders between his hands.

'Go on,' he commanded. 'What happened next? Did you go back to the pier to see who it was?'

'No, I swam to the beach and came back to the flat. I didn't miss my shoulder bag until I came to unlock the door.'

'Poor child!' He drew her against his chest. 'Were you very frightened?' He drew in a deep breath. 'I'd like to get my hands on whoever did it! You don't think it might have been a seagull? They dive-bomb the railway lines along the pier at night with mussels in order to crack them open for food.'

'I don't think so. I only saw one poised on top of one of the lights.' Suddenly Nora remembered the little plastic purse. 'It was an opening in the guard rail along the pier where I saw this purse. I went nearer to the edge of the space than I would have done normally to pick it up. It was near the edge of the pier as if someone had dropped it. I have it here.'

Juan took the purse she gave him and examined it in silence.

'Meant to lure you to the edge, no doubt,' he concluded grimly. 'Mind if I keep this?'

Nora looked at him disliking the confused feeling that close contact with him gave her.

'What do you want to keep it for?' she asked curiously.

But Juan refused to be drawn. 'I might find out who it belonged to,' was all he said.

'Do you think we ought to tell the police?'

He shrugged. 'What can they do? They'll probably put it down to hooligans on a last-minute romp before the pier closed. No, leave this with me, I'll make a few discreet enquiries.' A thought struck him. 'Does anyone know about it?'

'The porter of the flats. He thinks I dropped the bag accidentally into the sea. He's promised to send a friend to find the bag for me. It concerns him since I'd left my keys to the flat in it. I'm so grateful to you for finding it for me.'

'You can tell him that a friend found it for you.' He prowled around the lounge, gesturing for her to sit down. Then he draped himself against the frame of the door leading into the kitchen.

'I'm going to be around for the next few weeks or so, and I have something to suggest to you. I know it's the wrong time of the day to talk, but we have to do so. How do you feel about going along with the idea that there's something between you and me?'

'You mean pretend we're more than friends?'

'It might help.' He unzipped his parka and blew out a tortured breath. 'It's warm in here. Doesn't anyone turn the heat off?'

'It is off. I was going to suggest a cup of coffee,' Nora added with a smile.

Juan sloughed his jacket. 'I'd welcome a cup—been to a party. My throat is dry,' adding as he caught her wary look, 'And it isn't through over-drinking. Everyone today seems to be mad on curry and I hate the stuff.'

'Then my coffee should taste good even if it isn't. Sure you wouldn't like a can of beer? I've one or two in the fridge in case of company.'

Nora talked to him from the kitchen, marvelling at the ease in which they were talking to each other. Perhaps the magic in the air had something to do with his concern about her when he had arrived at the flat earlier on. She liked to think it was genuine and that he really did like her.

'I'll have the coffee,' he replied.

He came into the kitchen to carry in the tray for her, and he dwarfed the space by his presence. She refused to look up at him as she placed some biscuits on a plate to put beside the coffee on the tray. She went into the lounge to pull up the low table by two comfortable chairs and Juan put down the tray.

'As a matter of fact I was going to call on you later today,' he said, dropping down into his chair and watching her pour out the fragrant beverage. 'I'm taking Aimée to the fish farm and I was going to ask you to come with us.'

Her dainty eyebrows lifted. 'Why me? Why not Tricia?'

'The idea is to give Tricia a break from looking after her daughter,' he informed her coolly as he raised the drink to his lips.

'I see. But Aimée doesn't know me. Won't she be uncomfortable with a stranger?'

'She'll like you. I have a feeling that most young things like you. Older ones too.'

Nora held her cup daintily between pearl-tipped fingers.

'That's very nice of you, but you don't have to pay me compliments in order to persuade me to do something you want,' she assured him. 'After all, I do owe you a debt. You found my bag—which reminds me, I shall have to let the porter know.'

He said roughly, 'I don't expect anyone to repay me when I happen to do them a good turn. Coming with us in that frame of mind isn't going to do much good to Aimée. I want you to come with us because you want to, and not from a sense of obligation to me.'

Nora smiled impishly. 'I'll come on one condition—that you behave to us both like an uncle who's giving his two nieces a treat.'

'So there are to be conditions. Nothing doing.' Juan put down his cup after draining it thirstily. The slight thud coincided with a ring at the front door.

'Whoever can that be?' exclaimed Nora, putting down her cup.

'I'll go,' he said, and strode to the door along the short passage.

'Oh!' exclaimed the porter, taken aback by Juan opening the door. 'Are you all right, Miss Bain?' he called. 'The people in one of the neighbouring flats told me a man had come up without a key to the front door.'

Nora hurried to the door, knowing what it would look like to the porter as he faced a man in his shirt sleeves looking as if he had a right to be there.

'Quite all right, thanks,' she assured him. 'Mr Cregeen brought my shoulder bag—he found it.'

'Indeed? Intact?'

'Yes.' It was Juan who spoke, with a nonchalant ease which made the porter's attitude look stuffy and overbearing. 'But it was more important to me that I should find Miss Bain intact. You get my meaning?'

'Certainly. I was only checking. It's what I'm here for,' the porter said a little stiffly.

Juan smiled. 'I appreciate that, and thanks for looking after Miss Bain. Here's something to share between you and the friend you have sent to look for the shoulder bag, and thanks again.'

Notes changed hands and the porter took his leave, all smiles.

'Seems to me,' drawled Juan as they made their way back to the lounge, 'you'll not only be coming out with me today, you'll be accompanying me quite often in the near future, unless you want your name to be mud.'

Nora sighed. 'I see what you mean. It looks as though our date is on. What with me in my negligé and you in your shirt sleeves combined with the smell of coffee, the poor man could jump to any conclusions. We ought to have asked him in for a cup.'

'Not on your life,' he retorted with some emphasis. 'What, and have the man making a habit of it?'

The last remark gave Nora food for thought. Five minutes ago Juan was suggesting they have a mock affair; now he was taking over as if it was a real one. In all fairness she had to admit that he had done the right thing where she herself was concerned. He had pressed the point unknowingly that a girl did better with a man around to protect her.

She would have felt more unsettled had it been Jony, because there would have been an ulterior motive in the suggestion coming from him. He had a lot to gain if he could turn the affair between them into the real thing, with a wedding ring.

She asked, 'Another coffee?'

'I don't mind,' answered Juan, dropping back into his chair.

Nora passed his coffee and poured another for herself to give her something to do. The white silk shirt he was wearing contrasted attractively with his tanned skin and dark crisp hair. There was an attractive aura about him that would persist even when he was ninety, she thought wryly.

'Your way of life must be very pleasant when it gives you the time to be knight errant to ladies in distress,' she said sweetly.

He laughed, amused at her sudden wary expression. 'I don't make a habit of it. I'm enjoying my present role of helping Aimée.'

'Only Aimée?' she asked.

He raised an eyebrow. 'And Tricia, if you like.'

'And me?'

He sipped his coffee, then surveyed her lazily.

'You aren't in need of much help. You have a delightful flat, a car, a share in a bequest—a generous one—and a good promising career.'

Piqued with something more than just disappointment, she snapped, 'Thanks!'

Juan gave the slow smile which always played on her heartstrings. 'I might add that you've been richly endowed with nature's decorations too—but I won't enlarge on your charms. I'm sure you're aware of them.'

Her face went scarlet. 'You can be a very aggravating man, do you know that, or do you delight in needling people?'

'It keeps the adrenalin going,' he scoffed. 'I'd like to bet Jony's gets working when he sees us together.'

She picked up his trend of thought immediately. 'You mean because you're a Manxman he might think...?'

'Exactly. That he stands to lose half the income on the estate if we marry.'

'Oh dear, I never thought of that! There's something else too. If... if someone made an attack on me because of the will won't... they try it again now that there's a real threat to Jony inheriting the lot?' she said, aghast.

'I wouldn't worry about that if I were you. I shall be around most of the time and the porter seems a nice dependable sort. You're not scared, are you?'

He emptied his coffee and leaned forward to take her hand. Nora had put down her coffee cup with trembling fingers, and he had noticed it. His tone softened.

'Look, there's nothing to be scared of. I think I know who dropped the plastic purse and it's some-one who won't bother you again. I'm saying no more; you must take my word for it. Will you trust me?'

Nora's fingers curled around his, anxious for their reassuring warmth.

'I'll have to, won't I? I've no other option,' she told him flatly.

The attractive smile was on his dark face again. 'You won't feel so bad when you know me better. Come on, smile!'

That's the trouble, she thought. Knowing you better will bring other problems. She walked to the door with his arm resting carelessly around her shoulders. His right arm was crooked to carry the jacket on his shoulder.

'Pick you up at two,' she said.

Juan was on time; so was Nora. Aimée was seated in the front seat of the car beside Juan. Nora had a first impression of big eyes in a small heart-shaped face regarding her solemnly. Blonde hair curled in silky tendrils around the small features reminiscent of Tricia's. Her smile and her blue eyes were shy and lacked the hardness of her mother.

'Juan has been telling me about you,' she said shyly as Nora settled herself in the back seat of the big car. 'I knew I'd like you,' she smiled as Nora leaned forward in her seat. 'I always like Juan's friends.'

With a flippancy she could not feel, Nora said, 'Liking a person can go a long way in being real friends. I hope you'll be my friend, Aimée. You have a very pretty name.'

'It belongs to a very pretty girl,' Juan put in as he started the car.

Aimée looked at him adoringly. 'Juan always says nice things and he never says anything he doesn't mean.'

'That's nice to know,' Nora put in dryly.

The journey to the fish farm was not a long one, and the weather was just right for a visit into the countryside. The scenery along quiet leafy roads was bright with sunlight when Juan parked the car near to the entrance of the fish farm.

Aimée loved the huge stone toads at the entrance and inside the fishing farm. To their right as they entered was the souvenir shop, while to their left immediately behind them was the shed which housed the stages of the breeding from minute specks to fully grown fish.

One of the young men in charge met them as they emerged from the shed with a yellow plastic pail which he offered to Aimée. It contained brown pellets of food for the fish.

'Would you like to feed the fish for me?' he asked with a smile.

She shone up at him with delight as delicate colour suffused her small face.

'May I?' she cried delightedly.

There were four rectangular pools containing the fish in various stages of their development, ranging from small ones to the fully grown rainbow trout. Aimée went around the pools feeding the smaller ones before reaching the end product.

The fish came in swarms to the surface of the water to be fed, snatching the small brown pellets very quickly. Juan had brought his camera to produce instant coloured pictures and he took several of Aimée feeding the trout as they leapt high from the water in all their beautiful colours.

He also took pictures of Nora as the two golden heads came together as they leaned over the edge of the ponds to gaze with pure delight at the leaping rainbow trout.

'Aren't they lovely pictures?' cried Aimée, devouring the snaps with delighted gaze.

For an instant, Nora met Juan's gaze over the child's bright head and her smile became fixed as their eyes collided. She tore her gaze away, but not before her heart had done a swallow dive in her breast. What a romantic idiot she was, to allow herself to be affected by his kindness to a child!

By the time they reached the place Juan had chosen for their picnic Nora had control of her emotions and decided to hold them in check in the future. The picnic box contained everything to delight the heart of a child, including flasks of iced fruit drinks, hot coffee, sandwiches, cakes, biscuits and a whole chicken which they shared between them.

After their picnic they played with a ball on the grass in the small leafy hollow with only the birds for company. Then they flung themselves down to rest and soon Aimée was asleep. Nora was conscious of the long form of Juan stretched out not far away from her and the child. She tried to shut him out by closing her eyes, but the dark head, the wide shoulders tapering down to narrow hips, affected her profoundly. It had been a mistake to come out with him. As for anything concerning a more intimate relationship, it worried her.

He said quietly, 'Glad you came?'

'Who wouldn't be? It's a beautiful place.'

'But you aren't relaxed, are you? Still worried about the incident on the pier?'

She turned her head to meet his eyes. 'Not really.'

His eyes narrowed over the lightly tanned clear

skin overlaid by a pink bloom, the clear, curly-fringed eyes, and the silky golden hair lifting tantalisingly in the faint breeze. Her pink mouth was unsmiling, but very tempting had she but known it.

'You know,' he began with a gentle taunting look, 'you'd be quite a girl once you let yourself go. How do you get on with this partner of yours? Ever thought of taking him on in the marriage stakes?'

'No. We're good business partners, that's all. Why do you ask?'

'Because I would have that in mind if I'd been in his shoes. Does that surprise you?'

'It does,' she replied dryly. 'Especially since you confess to preferring the single state.'

'I never said I preferred it, merely that I enjoyed my life as it is at the moment.' Juan laughed as if at some private thought. 'What heading does your company go under—Bain, something and Company?'

'That's right. My name is first since it was my father's business, but I can see you wouldn't tolerate that for long if you were the partner. You just wouldn't stand for a woman being first.'

'No, I wouldn't. I'd toss her for it.' He grinned. 'Oh, come on, smile! You know, in the position you're in with the stiff upper lip keeping the old firm going, you're heading to be one of the most hard-bitten females in the business. What have you got against men?'

'What do you mean?' she demanded in a voice as steady as she could make it.

'What I say.' His second appraising glance had a sharpness in its depths. 'You have this sophisticated look which clearly tells all comers to keep their distance—men, that is. Don't get me wrong, I'm not against sophistication in women, I regard it as a part of their feminine charm. It's tantalising if you don't use it as a shield.'

'Perhaps, like you, I enjoy my life as it is.' She wished he wouldn't take that older brother attitude each time he addressed her.

'Being on your own?'

'Why not? You do.' Nora eyed him balefully. 'I'm not meddling with your life. Why meddle with mine?'

'I wouldn't agree,' he said slowly. 'Meddling is hardly the word I would use. Invasion, perhaps.'

'Invasion? In what way have I invaded your privacy?'

'You'd be surprised. Anyway, this is neither the time nor the place to go into such matters.' Juan consulted his wristwatch. 'Another half an hour and Aimée will be going back. I don't want to tire her too much. She's doing fine, especially since coming to the island. Aimée is one of the lucky ones in getting well so quickly after an attack of polio. Incidentally, I may be taking her for a sail one of these days. What do you say about coming with us?'

'What about Tricia?'

'Tricia has other fish to fry. Besides, I'd better take you since we're to work up a relationship.' He held up a hand to prevent the protest parting her lips. 'And for heaven's sake don't look as if I'd suggested something improper! We shall have Aimée with us.'

'Nora cast a glance at the sleeping girl. 'Can she swim?' she asked thoughtfully.

'Not very well. Her limbs aren't back to their usual freedom of movement, but she's trying.'

'Poor darling,' she said on a deep sigh.

'Does that mean you'll come sailing with us?'

'I'll let you know,' she said. A sudden thought struck her. 'Where did you find my shoulder bag? On the beach? Was it washed up?'

Juan smiled. 'The strap had wrapped itself around the pier. Comes in useful, doesn't it, that pier—in more ways than one?'

Nora quelled a shudder.

'Hey now,' he said with concern, 'there's no need for you to be afraid anything more will happen, so forget it.'

'I wish I could believe you.'

'You can,' he told her forcefully.

CHAPTER FOUR

NORA spent the evening alone, from sheer cussedness rather than from choice. On the way back from the fish farm Juan had asked her again, this time in front of Aimée, to go with them for a sail at some future date. With the child's eyes fixed on her face in silent poignant appeal Nora had reluctantly agreed. But she had refused to make any dates with Juan in the meantime.

So when the doorbell rang that evening at seven she went to answer it expecting Juan to be there. She wanted him to be there, although she did not know what she would say to him. It was not his way of ringing the bell, but he could have been deliberately ringing it differently in case she did not answer it when she recognised it.

She had not dined but had changed her dress for the evening, just in case Juan came.

'Hello there,' Jony greeted her sheepishly. 'I thought I'd call to see how you were faring.'

Nora found herself greeting him just as awkwardly. 'Hello, Jony. Nice of you to call. Do come in,' she added on a late smile.

He came in and followed her to the lounge.

'Come in,' she repeated as he stood awkwardly in the doorway. 'And sit down. I'm fine. How are you?'

He looked at her warily as he took a chair and she sat opposite to him in the other.

'Fine,' he answered laconically. 'Going out much?'

'Yes. I have the car and I go swimming.'

'Go along the pier?'

'Sometimes.' Nora hesitated, seeing his closed look. Had he heard about the incident on the pier. Was that the reason for his visit? If he had anything to say on the matter he left it unspoken. She moved uneasily in her chair, reluctant to say anything about it. It was something she preferred to forget. 'Would you like a cup of coffee or something?' she added lamely.

He shook his head and said awkwardly, 'I only called to see how you were going on.'

Nora frowned and gave a pained smile. 'You said that as if you were expecting something to happen to me.'

He rose awkwardly to his feet, and mumbled, 'You being a girl on your own and inheriting what you have are points always open to speculation.'

She said pointedly, 'You mean having someone seeking my company with that in mind? I'm beginning to see what you mean now by everybody here knowing everything about what goes on. Have you come to warn me about anything or anyone in particular? If you have just tell me. I don't think it's necessary because I can take care of myself. But since you're here . . .'

Jony moved slowly across the room as though deep in thought. Her plain speaking had obviously taken him aback and Nora wondered what was going on beneath that closed exterior.

He was at the door when he spoke. 'I'd be careful of going out with strangers if I were you,' he said darkly.

Nora followed him to the door. 'By strangers you mean Juan Cregeen?'

His face went a dull red. 'I wouldn't trust him if I were you.' He gestured towards the sea with his head. 'That yacht out by the pier isn't his. It belongs to a millionaire. You'll always find Juan Cregeen among the people with money.'

'I've met the millionaire,' she told him sweetly. 'Finn Cullan. He seems a nice man.'

He shrugged. 'Can't say I've heard anything bad about him, but you can't be too careful these days.'

He had washed and changed into a presentable suit, and Nora presumed that he was about to go out with his girl-friend or spend an evening in one of the pubs.

She agreed. 'Thanks for callling,' she said, walking past him along the short corridor to the front entrance of the flat, and opening the door. 'See you around.' Her smile was friendly, but she knew he shared the tension inside her. Somehow they never quite shared that ease of manner which was an integral part of friendship between two people.

When he had gone Nora returned to the lounge with mixed feelings. His visit had unsettled her and she prowled around the room, wishing she knew what was at the bottom of his visit.

She was staring aimlessly through the window when two figures walking along the promenade by the sea wall caught her attention. There was no denying the wide-shouldered, slim-hipped grace of Juan Cregeen and the more bulky form of Finn Cullan.

Nora willed them to look up at her flat, but they did no such thing. They were going towards the pier, presumably to the yacht anchored there. Both wore parkas and were bareheaded. She drew in a frustrated breath, swung round, and snatching up a wrap and her evening purse, she left the flat.

It was imperative for her to get out of the flat and she made for the restaurant adjoining. The meal was good, might have been excellent had she been in the mood for it.

The man who asked politely if he could share her table was the elderly type with a roving eye, but Nora was not bothered. Apparently his son had a yacht in the harbour and they spent most of their time there. His son had another engagement that evening, so he was on his own.

He began by asking her about herself, but gave up when she made it clear that sharing her table did not mean he was entitled to know anything about her, and began to talk about the island. When the meal was over he suggested a stroll along the promenade because it was such a lovely evening. Nora agreed, feeling grateful for his company, and they stood by the sea wall looking across at the three yachts anchored by the pier.

Her companion said, 'That yacht nearest the pier, the *Dancing Belle*, belongs to Finn Cullan. Nice boat.'

But Nora merely murmured something and when he suggested a stroll along the pier she said she was going indoors.

'Thank you for your company,' she said, turning to him with a smile. 'We were both at a loose end and it's been a pleasant interlude.'

He raised a calculating brow. 'What about a nightcap?'

'No, thank you.'

'What about an evening out tomorrow? There's a good eating place over at the . . .'

'I'm sorry. As I said, we were both at a loose end. Let's leave it at that, shall we? Goodnight.'

He shrugged thick shoulders. 'No chance of a future date? The island can be lonely when you're on your own.'

She shook her head. 'Sorry.'

Again he shrugged. 'Are you in a hotel?' he persisted.

'I'm staying with a friend.' If one could call the ghost of Jed Kelly that, she thought.

'Goodnight, then,' he answered. 'Can't blame me for trying.'

Back in the sanctuary of her flat Nora pulled the draw curtains to shut out what was for her the turbulence of a calm night. She wondered if Juan and Finn were sleeping on the yacht and felt comforted by the thought of them being near.

The next day the island was covered with the thick mist of incessant rain. All day long the skies were laden and dark, and the sea had white horses topping mountainous waves. Nora went to Douglas in the car, browsed around the shops and had lunch there. It was late afternoon when she was putting the car back in the garage and the rain was still coming down.

Pulling the hood of her white mackintosh over her bright hair, she went to the corner of the flats to peer across to see if the Dancing Belle was still there. It was.

The next day was dull, rainless but stormy at sea. Nora dined in the flat that evening and later went for a stroll through the quiet little village. The main street was almost deserted except for cars passing through. Several people were taking their dogs for their evening stroll, their owners gazing through the windows of shops long since closed for the night.

Turning the corner to enter the glass-fronted entrance to the flats, Nora stopped precipitately. A tall, broad-shouldered figure was leaning negligently against the wall waiting for her. The ground beneath her feet seemed to rock as she pushed open the glass door.

The yachting cap was pushed back on the dark crisp hair and his hands were thrust into the pockets of his jacket.

'Juan,' she croaked huskily. 'What are you doing here?'

'Waiting for you.'

His eyes were steady and enigmatic. He looked strong and vital and it made Nora feel weak just to look at him.

'Waiting for me?' she echoed. 'Why?'

'To make arrangements for our sail tomorrow.'

'Are we going sailing?'

'The weather is going to be nice tomorrow. The storm has blown itself out. Put a warm sweater on and bring a mackintosh with hood, that's all.'

'All?' she cried, repeating him like a parrot. 'What if I've made other arrangements?'

'Cancel them. You don't want to disappoint Aimeé, do you? She's never stopped asking when we are going.'

'You could always take Tricia,' she prevaricated.

She tried to collect her wits in order to subdue the sudden surge of emotion his unexpected appearance had caused.

'What's the matter? Scared? I'll turn back at the slightest sign of bad weather. That's the only thing that need bother you.' His lip curled a little as he spoke.

Nora knew he was cutting her down to size. At the same time he was making it very difficult for her to wriggle out of a promise, however reluctantly it had been given.

'What time?' she asked, avoiding his eyes.

'Ten o'clock. We can go along the pier in the little train. Aimée will enjoy it and it will give her a much-needed lift to the jetty to board the boat.'

His eyes roved over her face glowing from the fresh air, the clear eyes were shining. She looked as slender and fresh as a young willow.

He grinned, his teeth white against his tan.

'You'll be going back home looking as fit as a fiddle when we've finished with you!'

'That's very comforting,' she assured him with a bite of sarcasm. 'But I don't happen to have had polio.'

'You can thank the Lord that you haven't,' he answered grimly. 'I hope to heaven you never do.'

Nora bit on her lip. 'Then stop treating me as if I had,' she snapped. 'Honestly, the way you treat me, anyone would think that I was Aimée's twin sister!'

'I could treat you like a grown-up,' he said darkly. 'But therein lies the danger. Still, if that's what you want...'

'Oh, stop trapping me into corners,' she cried angrily. 'I've never met anyone like you!'

'That makes two of us. Interesting, isn't it? Have you missed me?'

Nora pushed past him and inserted her key in the lock of the hall door.

'Goodnight,' she said without turning round.

Juan's deep chuckle followed her to the elevator. Why with all the island to choose from did she have to meet such an aggravating, impossible young man?

Nora was waiting for Juan and Aimée the following morning when they called to pick her up. The man who drove the little train had not turned up, so Juan got the train ready himself and drove them down to the landing steps. He lifted Aimée on to his back, carried her down the steps to the waiting dinghy, then put her and Nora into it.

Tremors ran through Nora when Juan lifted her aboard the *Dancing Belle*. She saw white teeth glistening beneath the peaked cap as he steadied her with his hands on her waist until she had the feel of the boat.

'There isn't much of either of you,' he said.

'You're like two pieces of thistledown.'

The morning was perfect for sailing when Juan cast off from the buoy. Down below Aimée was excited about her first sail.

'It's great,' she said, hugging Nora. 'I'm going to marry Juan when I grow up.'

Her hair was in a ponytail. She wore jeans and a striped sweater in navy and white and there was a red ribbon in her hair.

Nora teased, 'I bet that's why he hasn't married,' holding the small head against her.

Aimée looked up at her seriously. 'You don't think he'll marry anyone else, do you?' She sighed. 'He's so very attractive. Of course, I wouldn't mind if he married someone like you—until I grow up. Then I'd want him back.' Nora was laughing when Juan joined them.

'Am I missing something?' he asked, looking from one to the other with a cocked eyebrow.

'Don't tell him, Nora.' Aimée giggled, but her look at him was openly adoring. 'I'm thirsty. Please can I have a drink?'

Juan eyed her darkly. 'So it's to be two to one, is it?' He ruffled her hair. 'Well, I would remind you, miss, that I'm the strongest of the three of us. Also I have you both at my mercy, so beware!'

Aimée laughed as he handed her a glass of orange juice and a packet of chocolate biscuits. Then he went in the galley to make coffee.

Aimée had made short work of her drink and several chocolate biscuits when Juan brought in the coffee. He gave a cup to Nora and sat down with his opposite to her on the padded cockpit side seats.

Aimée nibbled another biscuit. 'I wish we could do this every day,' she said wistfully.

'You'd soon get bored,' Juan told her lazily.

'I would never get bored with you,' she assured

him earnestly. 'Tell me another story about the fairies on the island.'

Juan grinned. 'They'd soon be fed up with your incessant chatter for a start. They can't stand noise. All fairies have a great objection to noise. It's said that three score and ten years ago a man was wakened from his bed on a fine spring morning to the murmur of voices outside his window. Going to look, he saw an orderly procession of hundreds of the little people scrambling over stepping stones in the river to make their way slowly up the Bearey Mountain until they disappeared in the mist at the top. Most of them wore tiny pointed caps on their heads and were carrying pots, pans, kettles and even spinning wheels, all their worldly possessions. A mill had recently been built in the village and they objected to the noise it made. So they went in search of a quieter place.'

Aimée clapped her hands as Juan finished his coffee. As he put down his cup Aimée threw herself at him to kiss him soundly.

'Now tell Nora a story—please, Juan,' she begged.

He looked startled at the suggestion. 'I'm sure Nora has no such childish fancies.'

'Oh, but I'm sure she believes in the fairies, don't you, Nora?' Aimée's big eyes were very appealing.

Nora laughed, avoiding Juan's mocking eyes. 'Indeed I do,' she said lightly. 'I'm not sure that Juan does, though.'

'Of course he does. Don't you, Juan? Go on,' Aimée urged, 'tell Nora a story.'

He laughed and tweaked her hair. 'I don't have to tell Nora a story to entertain her.'

The hesitancy in his voice made Nora look directly at him. He had pushed the yachting cap to the back of the crisp curling hair. His tall wide-shouldered frame dwarfed the confines of the cabin and she was once again reminded of that deadly charm. Furthermore, the remark he had made about being the strongest of the three of them came back to taunt her, for he was looking at her in much the same way that a pirate of old would look on a pretty captive.

Until now she had resented him treating her in the same category as Aimée, and the thought occurred that he had done so deliberately in order that, in her resentment, he would find the excuse he needed to treat her differently. But how differently? Could there be an easy camaraderie between them? She doubted it. There was too much chemical reaction on her part.

Nora put her cup down carefully. Juan Cregeen could try what tactics he liked, but he would discover that Nora Bain was not fair game.

'I'd love to hear a story of the island,' she said coolly. 'What kind had you in mind for me?'

Her attitude seemed to amuse him. He lifted a provocative dark brow.

'What about me telling the story of one Nora Cain?' he replied mockingly.

'Nora?' she echoed inanely.

He drew Aimée between his knees and his keen look across the space over her head cut Nora down to Aimée's level.

'It's said,' he began, 'that there's a submerged island near to Port Soderick which rises to the surface every seven years. This beautiful island was confined to the depths of the sea by a powerful magician named Finn MacCoul. He cast a spell on it and sent it to the bottom of the sea along with all the inhabitants whom he turned into blocks of granite.

'He did it because the inhabitants insulted him and by way of revenge he allowed it to come to the

surface every seven years for half an hour only. If in
that time while it surfaced someone were to place
a Bible on it then the enchantment would be
broken and the island would remain above the
water.

'Nora Cain had heard the story from her grandfather and it had made a deep impression upon her.
So one evening when she was strolling in the bay
with her lover she saw something rising slowly
out of the sea. As it rose higher she recognised it as
the enchanted island and, rushing back to her home,
grabbed a Bible, to the consternation of her parents.

'After explaining what she wanted it for Nora
ran back to the bay just in time to see the island
gradually sinking again from sight. She was so disappointed at being too late to save the island that
she lost all interest in life and she eventually pined
away and died. Her heartbroken lover followed her
soon after. Nobody else has ever looked out for the
enchanted island since, because they feared the
wrath of the magician might backfire on them by
making the Isle of Man disappear in the same way.'

Aimée said solemnly, 'That's a very sad story,
but I like it. Do you know any more stories, Juan?'

He laughed. 'Hey, we've come on a sail, remember? Come on, let's go on deck for some fresh air.'

As he rose to his feet Nora rose too. 'I'll wash the
cups and things,' she said hurriedly.

Juan instantly placed a restraining hand upon
her arm.

'You will not,' he said firmly. 'Up on deck with
you.'

Aimée looked up at them both and said primly,
'You didn't thank Juan for telling you the story,
Nora.'

Nora gazed down at Juan's hand on her arm and
her face grew warm.

'Thank you, Juan,' she said without lifting her eyes.

'Don't mention it,' he answered.

'Aren't you going to kiss him?' queried the irrepressible Aimée.

Nora's colour deepened into a creamy rose. Still not looking at Juan, she said, 'Grown-ups don't go around kissing people for bringing them on a sail, or for telling them a fairy story.'

'Oh, but they do,' Aimée insisted. 'They do it all the time where we live. You ask Mummy. They say thank you, darling, then kiss them.'

Juan chuckled at her perfect imitation of someone she had obviously seen.

'You're a little horror,' he said grimly.

'I'm not, I'm not!' she cried. 'Just because you're afraid to kiss Nora you're blaming it on me.'

Nora felt by now that the whole situation was getting out of hand. Yet she felt hypnotised by his grip on her arm and his nearness was suffocating. He was either drawing her closer or she was leaning his way.

The next moment his arms went around her and he bent his head. The cabin spun around her in a wonderful exhilarating feeling of having suddenly come to life. Aimée was forgotten in the joy of soaring to the heights of bliss in Juan's arms.

Lost in long moments of esctasy, Nora came to earth when Aimée said plaintively, 'I thought we were going on deck.'

'Off with you, then.'

Juan's down-to-earth command came as he released her, just as if nothing had happened, Nora thought resentfully. A kiss was nothing to him; he had merely been playing along with Aimée. As for herself, she knew he had taken something from her that would be his for always.

It was her fault; she could have drawn back instead of letting him have his way. But the harm was done, and for the rest of that day she never really looked at him. Aimée was tired out when they returned to anchor the boat near to the pier. The man in charge of the pier was waiting for them and Juan's car was there. The miniature train had been put away, so the man had driven Juan's car along the pier to meet them.

He was obviously pleased at the tip Juan gave him before they drove away, for he waved them off with a grin.

'What about coming to spend the evening with us?' Juan asked as they neared her flat.

'No, thanks. I've enjoyed the day out,' Nora replied, and he did not attempt to change her mind.

Aimée was fast asleep in the back seat and Nora sat in front with Juan.

'I hope another visit to the pier has cleared your mind of the unpleasant incident of the other evening,' he said as he stopped the car outside the entrance to her flat.

She hesitated and quelled a shudder, having noticed that the gap on the pier through which she had been pushed had been filled.

'Not exactly,' she answered. 'After all, the mystery hasn't been cleared up.'

'It has,' he answered. 'I'll tell you about it some time, but not now.' They sat for a moment or so in silence, then he said, 'Thought any more about improving our friendship? I don't want you to spoil your holiday by unnecessary fears.'

Nora swallowed on a lump in her throat. The temptation to have him take care of her was great but foolhardy. As things were it was quite possible for her to go away and forget all about him, but not if she strengthened the bonds between them. That way was madness.

The familiar smart figure of the man waiting for her at the entrance to the flats opened her eyes to their fullest extent. There was no time to dwell on what he was doing there; it was sufficient that he was there at a most convenient moment.

'Floyd!' she cried, flinging herself from the car. 'What a surprise! What on earth are you doing here? Why didn't you tell me you were coming?'

Floyd Renner took her hands in his and grinned down into her delighted face.

'I thought I'd come to see what you were up to. You look blooming. Been out for the day?'

His eyes roved over her tousled appearance, the bright disarranged hair, the clear eyes and laughing red lips.

'I've been for a sail. Let me introduce you, Juan...'

Her voice trailed off as she turned to where she had left Juan in the car. He had gone.

'Make yourself comfortable.' Nora indicated the lounge while she turned to her bedroom. 'Help yourself to a drink in the cabinet while I wash and change.'

Really, she thought irritably, Juan might have waited to be introduced! Then she pushed him to the back of her mind and took a quick shower. Floyd was sitting comfortably reading the morning newspaper which Nora had left on the low table by his chair.

'No drink?' she asked, coming gracefully into the room and looking for a glass by his elbow.

'I was waiting for you,' he told her, looking at her with undisguised appraisal.

Her housecoat, in pastel shades of silk nylon, fell in soft full folds from an Empire bodice and short stand-up collar. Her golden floss-silky hair formed a light halo around her head and her dark brown eyes looked velvet-soft in the peach bloom tan of her face.

'I forgot how lovely you are,' he said slowly, 'and I mean that as a compliment. The air seems to suit you here—or is there another reason for this show of glowing health and beauty?'

She laughed and went to get him a drink. 'Why don't you stay and find out?' she asked. 'And I don't believe you've come out of curiosity.'

She gave him his drink and laughed down at him. 'Would you prefer to eat out? I've some cold chicken and salad in the fridge. I can rustle up a decent meal if you care to stay in.'

He took the drink. 'I have a room here at the adjoining hotel. I'll go for a bottle of wine.'

'Then while you're out I'll prepare the meal.'

Floyd sipped his drink and looked around the flat. 'Nice place, this, and all your own. Unbelievable! You do intend to come back, don't you?'

She took his empty glass. 'What makes you think I won't?'

He straightened and buttoned his jacket. 'The big car and the handsome chauffeur just now who brought you home to the flat. Was it that Jony fellow?'

'No, it wasn't—and he's no chauffeur. That was a yachting cap he was wearing.'

'Nice car,' he commented. 'I noticed it had a U.K. registration. He isn't Manx, I presume?'

'He's visiting the island on business. You might meet him later,' she answered, and blessed her sudden rise in colour.

'I'll fetch a bottle of wine,' he said dryly. 'I'll probably bump into him if he's in the habit of hanging around.'

'He isn't,' she replied, and he left on a shrug of non-committance.

Nora began to get the meal with an uneasy feeling of trouble in the shape of cousin Floyd. He had come bringing problems and she had more than enough of her own to contend with.

'Business all right?' she asked as they ate the delectable meal.

'Excellent,' he replied, taking a piece of chicken breast and washing it down with wine. 'About the offices? The ones I wrote to you about. Have you thought it over about us moving?'

'No, I haven't—I've more important things on my mind at the moment. Do you realise that in order to inherit part of the vast income from Mr Kelly's estate I have to marry a Manxman?'

He looked remarkably unruffled. 'Well, why not? You can always make it a marriage of convenience.' He snapped his fingers. 'Get an annulment.'

'Just like that?' she cried indignantly. 'I couldn't do that to poor Mr Kelly!'

'He won't know, will he?' he said philosophically.

'That doesn't make it right.'

'Then what are you going to do? Think it over? If you are you might give me an answer regarding the new offices I mentioned,' he pushed.

She gave him a brief unyielding stare. 'I happen to be more than satisfied with what I have, the flat, and the car. But I want to do what Mr Kelly wanted me to do,' she countered.

'Then there's your answer. Do what he wants you to do. What does this Jony think about it?'

'He has a girl-friend he's been courting for ten years.'

He gave a low whistle. 'Are they living together?'

'Not that I know of.'

He eyed her calculatingly. 'I'd say you could have

a number of suitors after your fortune. Shall you still want to carry on with the old firm?'

'That's a fool question,' she snapped. 'Of course. You can sell my car if you like. I shall bring my new car back with me.'

'Selling your car will present no problems. I've missed you.'

Floyd pushed back his empty plate as a hint for Nora to get up and take it away with her half-filled one to the kitchen. She was some time dishing up the apple pie and cream.

'You heard what I said,' he went on pointedly upon her return to the table with the tray. 'I missed you.'

Nora gave him a generous helping of the apple pie and added a dollop of thick cream.

'You mean you missed my cooking. All those evenings you came to dinner!'

He picked up his spoon and looked at her darkly. 'That isn't what I mean and you know it.'

Nora put a small portion of the apple pie on her own plate and an equally small amout of cream. Then she sat down and looked at him across the table.

'We have a good business partnership, but marriage is a very different matter. You and I have nothing in common except the shared enthusiasm for our job. As for new offices, we don't need them— certainly not the kind they're building now.'

'But we're taking on more responsibility. We need to expand,' he said stubbornly.

'So you keep saying.' Nora ate a portion of pie daintily. 'There's nothing that can't wait until I get back. Meanwhile, I have to concentrate upon the job in hand. Surely you can see that?'

'I can see you're being difficult as usual,' he answered in aggrieved tones.

Her mouth quirked at the corners. 'As usual meaning when you want your own way. We'll go into it when I come back. How long are you staying?'

'I was going back tomorrow. There's really no point in my staying,' he muttered sulkily.

'It's up to you. You might enjoy a day or two here.' Her smile became impish. 'Who knows, you might even vet one or two possible suitors for my hand.'

His lips thinned. 'I really believe you're enjoying it.'

'Oh, don't be stuffy,' she snapped. 'I'll make the coffee, then you can tell me what's been going on while I've been away.'

Floyd had papers in his pocket which he wanted her to sign. They dealt with business matters amicably, but Floyd's morose expression was never far from his face. It was a relief to Nora when he finally left and she went to bed bemoaning the fact that all her problems were related to men. They were not worth bothering about.

CHAPTER FIVE

FLOYD had gone back. Nora had taken him to the airport and was feeling rather lost on her return to the flat. The feeling of restlessness was back and after her evening meal at the flat she went for a walk along the promenade towards the pier.

She had not gone for a walk alone on the pier since the dreadful night when someone had pushed her into the sea. It bothered her, this fear she still had each time she thought about it. It had been a beautiful day and the evening was warm and without wind. The sea was tranquil and looking up from where she had stopped she could see two couples half way along the pier standing looking down into the water.

Partly to quell her fears and partly because the walk along it was so inviting, Nora took a deep breath and went in through the turnstile. On the pier the little train had been put away in its usual siding and she could hear someone tinkering with it as she passed. They were on the far side of the train so she could not see what it was.

Forgetting all about it, she strolled along, enjoying the fresh smell of seaweed and salt water. The two couples she had seen at the rails were now coming towards her, and looking ahead she could see no one. When they had gone she would be alone on the pier. They were quite a long way off yet and by the time they had passed by Nora would be well on to the other end of the pier ... alone. Hastily she glanced behind, but saw no one.

It was very quiet with only the occasional swishing sound of the sea swirling around the girders of the pier. Slowly the two couples advanced. They were quite young, hardly out of their teens, and they were holding hands. Nora could hear their voices now and soon they would be gone. But still she kept walking on. When they had passed she would turn around and follow them.

Steady now, she assured herself. What's the panic? Had not Juan told her that there was no longer any danger lurking for her on the pier? But what did she really know about Juan? Only that he looked dependable, and it was so easy to be taken in by appearances.

Nora's mouth went dry and her hands clenched in the pockets of her jacket as she walked on, her heart throbbing violently. The two couples were almost abreast of her now. Give them a minute or so to pass on, then she would turn round and follow them. If anyone was actually watching and waiting for her they would know that she had turned back because she was afraid of what might be waiting for her. But what did it matter what they thought? They were too despicable, whoever they were.

They had gone. Nora drew in a deep breath and took further paces forward. Now! She swung round on her heel to face the way along the pier that she had come and something hit her head on. She clutched whatever it was to save herself from falling and felt arms like steel bands going around her.

'Steady on!' Juan's deep voice, threaded with laughter, struck her ears like a gong. 'You've knocked the daylights out of me!'

Nora had closed her eyes and she was shaking from head to foot. The floor of the pier seemed hinged and she had the sensation of being swung around until she was giddy. But it was all in her imagination, for she was standing gazing up into Juan's laughing face.

Suddenly the twinkle in his dark eyes was taken over by a look of concern. His arms tightened around her as he stared down at her working face.

'Nora,' he said urgently, 'what's wrong? You're shaking. Are you all right?'

She dropped her head with her forehead against his chest, and stood speechless, held tightly against him. What was he doing so close behind her? Had he been following her? A shudder went through her and then she stood perfectly still.

'You frightened me,' she whispered. 'What were you doing so close behind me? Where did you come from?'

'Hey, you are upset, aren't you?'

She lifted her head and looked up at him, white-faced but not trembling any more.

'Can you wonder, when you frightened me so badly?' she cried indignantly.

'I frightened you?' He laughed. 'You scared me too. Whatever made you turn round so unexpectedly?'

'I ... I ... decided to go back,' she stammered. How could she tell him that she had been afraid of being on the pier on her own? He probably did not know what fear was. Besides, it would not do to let him know how frightened she had been. Suspicions crowded in on her and she loosened her grip of him slowly.

He scanned her expression with dark intelligent eyes.

'There's something else, isn't there? You thought I was creeping up on you? You silly child, you're worse than Aimée. Come on, I'll take you back to the flat. I have my car outside the pier.'

Nora allowed him to put an arm loosely about her slim shoulders, and they went back along the pier in silence. The short run to her flat was soon accomplished and he calmly took the key out of her hand to go up with her to her flat.

'I'm going to make you a drink of hot sweet tea, so put your feet up,' he said, pushing her gently down on the settee.

Pushing cushions behind her head, he lifted her feet up and took off her sandals. Then he went into the kitchen. His comforting warmth and vitality had done much for restoring her calm, but Nora was not convinced of his part in the whole affair. He was being so gentle and kind, but it was not enough. How could she be certain that it was not an act?

Wearily Nora closed her eyes. It had been quite a day, what with Floyd adding to her problems and now Juan again. It would be so easy to succumb to his charm when perhaps, for all she knew, he meant her harm. Her eyes were still closed when he came with the tea and she opened them to find him gazing down at her with an expression in his eyes which he quickly changed to one of concern.

'Come on, drink this up and you'll feel fine,' he said, placing the cup in her hands. 'It's sweet and hot.'

Drawing up one of the chairs, he sat facing her just an arm's length away bent forward with his strong arms along his thighs.

'All right, you were trying to prove something to yourself,' he said. 'What I don't understand is why, after the first shock of bumping into me, you didn't relax when you saw who it was.'

Nora avoided his eyes. 'I thought you were creeping up on me. I was tensed up, seeing myself all alone on the pier deliberately asking for another attack from... from someone who for some reason wants me gone.'

'You weren't alone on the pier, I was there. I happened to be tinkering with the train. It had

seized up earlier in the evening and I felt bound
to help out since the man who runs it had done
me several good turns including bringing my car
along for Aimée after our sail. I'd put it right and
was cleaning up when I saw you along the pier. You
must have passed me without either of us realising
it.'

'You could have called me,' with an uncertain
smile.

'I didn't want to alarm you, so I sprinted along
after you and gave you the shock of your young life.'
He grimaced apologetically. 'I didn't mean to. I'm
sorry.'

He reached out a hand to push the silky hair
gently back from her forehead and her heart light-
ened absurdly at his touch. Now that her pulse was
back to normal it was enough for the moment to
have him near, to have him regarding her keenly yet
with unusual gentleness.

The hot tea was bringing back the healthy pink
to her cheeks and she drank the rest of it with his
eyes upon her. Taking the empty cup from her, he
put it down on the low table nearby, then took one
of her hands in his. She felt the cool strength of
the fingers closing around her own and waited.

He went on, 'I ought to have told you before
about that evening on the pier, but I was hoping
it wouldn't be necessary. You see, everything has
been taken care of. You have nothing to fear any
more.'

'How can I believe that when I know none of the
facts?' she asked shakenly.

Juan said slowly, 'The facts are that Jony has a
half-brother whom everybody calls Paitchey—
Paitchey is the Manx name for child. You see,
Paitchey has the mentality of a boy of seven and
he's nineteen years old. He's been in a home since

the age of ten and Jony has him home every weekend. Normally Jony has him with him during that
period, but on this particular day he was busy on
the farm and let Paitchey go fishing off the pier
with several other teenagers. No doubt you would
meet them that evening on the pier.'

Nora swallowed convulsively as she recalled seeing the boys passing her on the pier. Her fingers
clung to his, and she nodded.

'Go on,' she whispered huskily.

He continued, 'The boys would see you long
before you saw them and they would probably tell
Paitchey teasingly that you were Jony's new girl-
friend from across the water. As Paitchey is Jony's
responsibility because he's the boy's only relative,
you can imagine what effect this teasing remark had
on him. Right away he would think you'd come
to take Jony away with you back across the water.
So he let the boys go on ahead on leaving the pier.
They wouldn't bother about him lagging behind
because there was only one exit and they would wait
for him there.'

'But he might have gone down the steps of the
pier by the jetty and got drowned,' she said.

Juan shook his head and smiled. 'Paitchey then
put down the plastic purse and unhooked the rope
from across the gap in the pier rail. Then he hid
and while you were picking up the purse and
peering over the side, which I presume you would
do, he pushed you over into the water.'

Her eyes were wide with horror. 'But I might
have drowned! What if I hadn't been able to
swim?'

He smiled. 'Paitchey would take it for granted
that you could swim. He can swim like a fish, and
he learned by being pushed into the water. He
would naturally take it for granted that you'd swim

ashore by the same process. He wanted to scare you into going back and leaving Jony alone.'

'I see.' She lowered her eyes to their clasped hands and felt the strength of his. 'How did you find all this out?'

'By making a few enquiries after working it out who would do that to you. I went to see Jony, showed him the purse, and he recognised it as one Paitchey had received at a party given at the Home where he was staying. He'd put some money in it for the boy the day previous. He said he would question him about it, which he did. Paitchey no longer had the purse and he admitted giving it to a pretty girl on the pier who'd come from across. We presumed he meant you as the boys who were with him swore that he'd talked to no one on the pier while he was with them.'

'I hope he won't be punished,' Nora said anxiously.

'No one will know about it, so it won't come to anything unless you want to bring charges.'

'I would never do such a thing!' she cried, adding as something occurred to her, 'So that was why Jony called on me that day we went to the fish farm. He didn't stay long—just called in to ask how I was and mentioned the pier.'

He raised a brow. 'Did you tell him what had happened?'

She shook her head. 'No, I didn't. He warned me against you. He told me that the *Dancing Belle* wasn't yours.'

Juan laughed goodhumouredly. 'Jony's a deep one. He was sounding you out about Paitchey. He'll be grateful that you aren't taking the matter any further. It's probably done some good, because Jony will take more care of Paitchey in the future when he has him to stay. I'm afraid you had the worst of it, my little eayn.'

Nora wrinkled a smooth brow. 'What does eayn mean?'

'Manx for lamb.'

He let go of her hand and patted it. 'Anyway, it's all over and you needn't be afraid of going along the pier again alone. All right now?'

He laughed into her face and Nora felt a tugging of her heart-strings. She was fine while he was there. It would be when he had gone that the pain would start. And he had no idea of it. He would go back to the yacht and immediately immerse himself in its needs. What did he care that Nora Bain, a silly little comeover, had succumbed to his charms along with many other girls?

Pride cooled her voice. 'I'm fine, thanks to you. I'm sorry about Paitchey. I wish Jony had told me about him, but I suppose he wanted to protect the boy. As far as I'm concerned it never happened.'

She bit hard on her lip, wishing she could say the same about meeting Juan.

'Can I get you a drink or something?' she added stiffly.

'No, thanks.' Juan was obviously trying to find the reason for her sudden coldness. 'You're in no condition to entertain anyone. Go to bed—and don't have any nightmares. I'll let myself out.' He paused at the door. 'Aimée is having a birthday soon. I hope you can come?'

She hesitated. 'Let me know when and I'll buy her a present.'

'You mean you won't be going?'

He raised a dark brow and she lowered her eyes against his scrutiny.

'I'll let you know,' she answered evasively.

'You'll probably have an invitation. Goodnight. Meanwhile if you have any further problems let me know. You can contact me at Finn Cullan's place, The Armitage.'

Juan's unexpected exit might not have been so bad, Nora decided, if he had not been so offhand about it. He had been patently unconcerned at her frozen mitt, as it were. The thought that there was nothing to stop her packing and going home made her pause momentarily before she got to her feet. Then she surrendered to weariness and made her way slowly to her bedroom.

The pristine freshness of her room filled with sunlight greeted her after a disturbed night. As she searched for clean underwear she mused that it was a pity that cares could not be shrugged off as easily as clothes. The memories of the previous evening still rankled, but the thing that hurt most was Juan's offhand attitude when he had left.

Nora spent the next few days exploring the island by car. It was a relief to get away from the *Dancing Belle* in the bay and the constriction of four walls in order to sort out her problems. But always on her return to the flat her heart would contract and her nerves go tense when she approached the promenade which she regarded as Juan's familiar territory.

Then one morning she met him. The early post had brought an invitation for Aimée's birthday party and she was thinking about it on going out for her morning paper. Juan was leaving the supermarket carrying a box of provisions.

He grinned at her over the top. 'Hello there,' he said carelessly. 'How are you?'

Her colour deepened as the moment eased, and she met his amused eyes with a smile. She answered his queries as to what she had been doing since they last met and heard with deep misgiving that

Aimée was looking forward to her coming to her birthday party.

She asked uncertainly, 'Are you taking the box to your car?'

Juan looked down at the provisions in his arms and frowned.

'Yes, it's right behind you in the square. Why?'

'Would you wait while I go back to my flat for Aimée's present? Maybe you would take it for me?'

'Anything wrong with your car?' he asked in clipped tones.

'No.'

'Then why not take the present yourself to the birthday party?'

Juan's tone was baffling—meant, she thought, to challenge her into accepting. But a compromise was too fraught with personal conflict for Nora.

'I'm sure Aimée will be too engrossed in her presents and other small guests to miss me.'

The fresh breeze frolicked in the silky hair at her temples and curved the denim skirt against her shapely figure. The eyes she raised to his had a hint of pleading in their depths and her cheeks burned.

His glance roved slowly over her, and the ironic line of his well cut lips smoothed out.

'Another pair of hands are always welcome when there are youngsters to look after, and it's a big house,' he said meaningly.

'That's not fair, you know,' she blurted. 'You're setting out deliberately to make me feel small and ... and mean, when it isn't that at all.'

'What is it, then? It can't be the fact that you won't like travelling back in the dark, since you know I should fetch you and bring you back.' His eyes narrowed. 'I take it the boy-friend has gone back?'

She said with spirit, 'He is not my boy-friend!

He's my business partner. I was going to introduce you, but you didn't wait.'

'I'm intelligent enough to latch on when I'm de trop,' he told her caustically. 'Has he gone back?'

'Yes, he has,' she admitted reluctantly. 'Don't let me keep you—that box looks heavy.'

'You aren't keeping me. I was wondering if I was keeping you.'

'You weren't. I was going to collect my morning paper,' she answered warily.

He eyed her curiously. 'Ever been to the Calf of Man?'

'Not yet, but I'm working my way around,' she replied frankly. 'I can see now why Mr Kelly bought me the car. You certainly need it to get about the island.'

He agreed. 'Not much fun seeing it on your own, though. I have to go to Port St Mary this morning. What about coming with me? We can go on to the Calf of Man.'

For a moment Nora was tempted to turn him down flat. Then she gave in to a new sense of caution which she had learned through dealing with him. Her continued refusal to have anything to do with him could cause her more trouble since he was a man who could not resist a challenge. Besides, she was not yet used to the south of the island and crossing the short journey to the tiny island would entail parking her car.

Knowing her own haphazard way of reaching places provided a reasonable excuse to go with him. It was not a kind of capitulation, she assured herself; it was common sense.

'Sounds interesting,' she said, still reluctant to follow a decision which she might regret.

Juan's voice had the quality of the cool breezes that favoured the north of the island.

'Maybe Jed Kelly's idea of giving you the car wasn't such a good idea after all,' he said crisply.

Nora's cheeks went hot. 'What do you mean?'

'Without it you would have to mix more in the community. At the moment I bet you're wishing like mad that you hadn't come here at all.' The smile did not reach his eyes. 'The way you behave with me gives the impression that you don't trust anyone—or is it only me?'

Her colour deepened. 'I don't know what you mean. What could I have done to give you that impression?'

'Plenty.' His smile tightened faintly and his voice was mocking. 'I might not look it, but I'm as sensitive as the next bloke, but I've learned to relax and it would be a good thing if you did the same.'

'I do relax as far as I'm permitted with you. You might not realise it, but you can be very disconcerting and unpredictable,' she said indignantly.

His smile widened. 'Why not? You can't say that it's a bad thing, since there's nothing like keeping the adrenalin going. At least you won't be bored with me.'

'I might find you very tiring. You aren't exactly restful to be with.'

'You're becoming a little confused,' he drawled. 'It's the clean fresh air of the island that knocks you for six. I'll pick you up in half an hour when I've taken these provisions to the boat.'

Nora was waiting for him when he drove along the promenade from the pier, and she slipped into the front seat of the luxuriously upholstered car. Before starting the car he glanced at her pretty green linen trouser suit and taking her beige woolly jacket along with a matching shoulder bag, he tossed them behind him onto the back seat. Then he said mildly,

'What happened to the bag I retrieved from the sea? Ruined, was it, or did you want to forget all about it?'

'A bit of both,' she answered, and added hurriedly, 'That doesn't mean I wasn't grateful for getting it back. I was, enormously, because of my keys and other things.'

'All your love letters were ruined, were they?' he teased.

'You should know, since you searched the bag,' she retorted.

'So I should.'

He laughed and shook his head at her, and it was a tremendous relief when he started the car and gave his attention to the road ahead. But Nora need not have worried. He drove expertly and at speed, slowing down each time they approached something of interest. He patiently explained every landmark which he thought would interest her.

On the way to Port St Mary Juan pointed out a Viking burial ground at Balladoole, then pulled up as they topped a rise to a panoramic view of Port St Mary and the great rock at Bradda Head in the background.

Juan left Nora in the car while he went to deliver a parcel to the Yacht Club, then they had an early lunch.

'Sure that's enough?' he asked, taking the container holding vegetables from her to transfer some to his plate.

He had frowned to see that she had put potatoes and vegetables on to her plate in small portions.

'I'm not a big eater,' she confessed.

'I'm not greedy myself, but I do eat enough to keep me going until my next meal,' he admitted sardonically. 'With your figure you've nothing to worry about.'

He put down the vegetable dish and picked up the sauce boat to pass it to her. What fine strong hands he had, she thought, and that look of imperturbability made her feel weak.

As she looked up to pass the sauce back her eyes collided with his and she looked down quickly at her plate.

'Nice restaurant,' she said by way of making conversation. 'I suppose you come here often?'

'I have been before,' he answered laconically. He gave her a long speculating look as he picked up his knife and fork. 'Are you sure you can't make up your mind what you're going to do about the will and then put it clear out of your mind? The thing is whether you want to give your share over to Jony or not.'

She nodded. 'Yes, I suppose it is. I wish it was as simple as it sounds. If I were to give it all over to Jony and he misused it I would always worry about it.'

'But you wouldn't know, would you, when once you've left the island, what he does with it?' he said reasonably.

'If a wrong is done and you don't know about it that doesn't make it right, does it?' She took a long breath and forked up some vegetables. 'It's so difficult to know what to do.'

'You could go back home and think about it. The problem might seem smaller at a distance,' Juan suggested.

He went on eating his lunch, big, vital, and sure of himself and what he wanted from life. It must be cosy to be in such a comfortable state of mind, Nora thought wryly. On the island among the company of the yachting set he was without doubt surrounded by presentable girls. He could probably have his pick of them, so why should he just settle for one?

She brought her mind back to her own problem, then shied away from it. Why spoil her day?

'What's Jony's girl-friend like?' she asked. 'Do you know her?'

'I've seen her. No doubt you have too. She has a friend in the same flats as you and goes to see her several times a week. The woman can't get out much. She has rheumatism in her feet and Cissy goes to give her heat treatment or something. She's small and dark, quite pretty. I can't see what she sees in Jony.'

'She must love him, to have waited so long.'

'Ten years?' He raised a dark brow in mocking disbelief.

Nora did not look at Juan's smile, but she knew the quality of it. He was mocking her romantic view of an extra long courtship and, worse still, the idea that love itself could have played a part.

Angry that her heart seemed to quicken its beat, she said evenly, 'Perhaps Jony is selfish in holding on to his present way of life. It's different for a woman. She wants a home and children.'

'Really?'

'Yes, really,' Nora retorted. 'I know women better than you because I happen to be one myself. I suppose if you ever decide to marry there won't be anything romantic about it. She'll have to be someone who will fit into your way of life.'

'What's wrong with that?' he demanded, sitting back into his chair after clearing his plate. 'Perhaps we ought to qualify that last remark by saying that it will be someone who fits in with my ideas what marriage should be.'

'So you do have ideas about marriage?' she scoffed.

She stared at him challengingly, caught a faintly mocking glint in the dark eyes and looked away.

'I know what it entails if it has to last the whole course. Been round this part of the island much yet?'

'Not much, apart from looking at the shops,' she answered guardedly.

'So you won't have seen the Chasms? We'll take them in on our way to the Calf of Man.'

She said, 'Wouldn't it be better to continue on our journey without any stops in between? It might rain.'

'It won't rain. The wind is in the wrong direction.'

Nora laughed weakly. 'You know all the answers, don't you? Look, I'm just bothered that I might be taking up more of your time, that's all.'

His eyes narrowed. 'I'm not the kind who would permit you to do that. You're stalling. Worse, you're getting all het up at the thought of being with me for longer than you thought. Relax.' He grinned. 'What about having an ice cream sweet to follow in order to cool you down?' He shook his head. 'You're the first girl I've had any difficulty with up to now. Usually I find them pretty amenable.'

'Define amenable.'

His lips twitched. 'I've got a right one here, haven't I? Look, lady, suppose you leave everything to me. What do you propose for a sweet? Something soft and gooey...?'

'Like romance?' Nora cut in. 'Or something ice-cold that numbs all feeling such as your approach to it?'

He grinned again. 'Well, I'm going for apple pie and cream, so work that one out.'

CHAPTER SIX

NORA'S impression of Port St Mary was one of Manx cottages and villas built at random in a picturesque cove. It was beautiful in its quaintness and she found it enchanting. Leaving the village behind, they drove up the hill to the high land of the Mull Peninsula at the southernmost tip of the island.

'The road to the Chasms,' Juan commented, turning the car on to a narrow lane to his left. Slowly they descended to a small grass plateau used as a car park where a peep over a wall revealed the magnificent stretch of coastline below. With Juan holding Nora's arm they descended down a slope of rough grass to a whitewashed house with two words painted on the side: The Chasms.

The coastal scenery was majestically grand, the cliff face split right down the centre from top to bottom by deep crevasses. The wild grandeur of the sea far below dashing itself against the base of Sugar Loaf Rock which lay immediately to their left off the small headland reminded Nora of the rugged coast of Cornwall.

Juan pointed out a promontory to the south of the coast known as Spanish Head where, it was said, a galleon of the Spanish Armada was wrecked, and through it all Nora felt herself relaxing. At Cregneish they stepped into a folk museum housed in a one-storied, whitewashed thatched-roof cottage with an open hearth, earth floor and peat-lined roof.

Juan's mouth quirked as Nora stared in fascination at the old Welsh dresser, rough earthenware and grandfather clock, and she smiled at him upon seeing the double bed in another room.

'Not much chance of sleeping in,' he commented, 'judging by the fishermen's nets, peat cutting tools, handloom and the collection of carpenter's tools.'

'I bet they were happy, though,' Nora said tenderly.

She was gazing up at him outside the cottage with the breeze lifting her golden hair and her face glowed. He took her arm on the way back to the car but did not speak.

'You've been very kind taking me around,' she told him. 'I feel like Aimée being taken sightseeing by a big brother.'

'Only I'm not your big brother. Why not regard me as I am—someone you've met on holiday—and relax.'

She said wistfully, 'I wish I could. I keep wishing that I'd come on holiday in time to see Mr Kelly before he died. I might have learned then what his wishes really were when he made his will.'

'You know what his wishes were. He makes them clear enough in his will.'

'I know that, but...'

He cut in impatiently. 'Going all maudlin over the man isn't good for you. He probably never regarded you at all as a person, merely as an appendage of your mother. It was your mother whom he remembered. No doubt the will was meant to forge some kind of link with her before he died. He was a practical man, by all accounts. It's left to you to do the best you can for yourself.'

The delicate colour rushed to her face. 'You're making it seem horrible and nasty! At least he loved my mother to the end.'

'How do you know?' Juan asked lazily.

They had reached the car and he leaned against it, eyeing her mockingly.

'Oh!' she cried indignantly. 'Do you have to be so horrible? Why do you have to make me like you one moment and heartily dislike you the next?'

'Now you're talking like Aimée,' he scoffed. 'If you're really concerned about Jed Kelly why not go to his farm if you want to know more about him? I'll take you there if you like.'

'No,' she replied quickly. 'No, thanks.'

'Then stop brooding. It isn't healthy. I thought better of you.' He opened the door of the car and helped her in. Then sliding in behind the wheel beside her he paused before starting the car. 'How do you regard me? As another Jony?' he added quizzically.

'Well, you're both Manxmen, and ...'

He said bluntly, 'I'm not wholly Manx. My father was, but my mother was a farmer's daughter from Sussex. I was born here and educated across the water.'

'Then you have ties in both countries,' said Nora.

'So have you, via Jed Kelly and your mother.'

'In that case you and I should get along fine. I wonder why we don't?'

He spoke roughly. 'We could if you would only relax. We'd better move on and enjoy ourselves if you can stand it.'

She giggled. 'I'm sorry. You're a good sport. I really am lucky to have you take me around. Tell you what—I'll buy you a drink when we stop again.'

He slanted a grin at her before starting the car. 'That should keep me in good spirits,' he said sardonically.

'Now you're laughing at me,' she cried indignantly.

'I'm not. It's just that I don't let any girl I take out pay for my drinks or her own.'

He braked at the main road and then accelerated.

Nora sat back in her seat and felt like a boxer going into her corner for further combat. Juan really was prickly and she wondered what she had done to offend him, apart from offering to treat him to a drink.

She told herself she would be glad when the day was over. However, later when Juan took her hand to help her over the rough places on the Calf of Man, she felt a foolish urge to cling to his hand. It came to her then with a pleasant sense of shock that she liked him even while she hated him, which did not make sense. It was all so matey that she could only ignore her feeling of bewilderment and accept the situation.

They had returned to the flat and Juan braked at the entrance to say smoothly, 'Care to go out this evening to a dinner and dance at one of the local hotels?'

Nora hesitated, and his glance as it roved over her was casual. The invitation had been given on an impersonal note, given in such a way that she could hardly refuse. He had given her an enjoyable day out and he no doubt wanted to end the evening on a festive note.

In any case, any time spent with Juan always made her feel restless for the rest of the day. So she might as well go out with him for the evening instead of trying vainly to put him out of her mind.

'Rather sudden, isn't it?' she stalled.

'I have the tickets. I was coming round to ask you if we hadn't have met this morning.' He smiled. 'I'll call for you at eight o'clock.'

Nora took her time getting ready for the evening, taking a leisurely bath, washing her hair and giving herself a facial. The result reflected in her mirror was pleasing. The nylon silk dress in cyclamen pink with its swathed bodice and shoulder straps was enchanting. Her hair was a golden silk cloud and her brown eyes, dark-lashed, held an eloquent appeal.

The ring at the intercom bell took her by surprise and she saw that it was only half past seven. Juan was early. But it was not Juan. It was her lawyer.

'Come in, Mr Garrant,' she said. 'This is quite a surprise.'

'Sorry to trouble you. I came this afternoon, but you were out, and as I was coming to the Viking Hotel this evening I decided to call again with your deeds for the flat.' He stared at her for a moment in appraisal, and smiled. 'You're going out too, I see. I won't be long settling our bit of business. Now let me see...'

He drew out a long bulky envelope from the inside pocket of his evening jacket and took out legal documents. The business of handing over the deeds of the flat was over and Mr Garrant was having a drink when Juan arrived.

He gave a low whistle of appreciation when Nora opened the door to him.

'You look and smell delicious,' he murmured. 'I can see I shall be busy keeping the wolves at bay.'

'We have company,' she told him, leading the way into the lounge.

'I know,' he answered. 'Evening, Richard,' he said to her guest.

Richard Garrant greeted Juan cordially. 'It seems we're all going to the same dinner.'

Nora looked from one to the other. 'I don't understand.'

Juan leaned nonchalantly against the wall of the small lounge. His lips twitched.

'Richard is staying as Finn Cullan's guest at the Armitage for the weekend. His wife is over on the mainland and Richard is hoping to enjoy some good fishing.'

'At the dinner and dance?' Nora asked, annoyed that she had not been told more about it.

There was a gleam of amusement in Juan's dark eyes as he drawled, 'Richard has done with that kind of fishing years ago.' He regarded her with deliberate intentness, taking in her pleasing figure in the pretty dress, and the creamy neck and shoulders it revealed. 'I didn't know Richard was coming to stay for the weekend until I got back after leaving you and Finn told me.'

A wave of colour spread over her cheeks at the way he had read her thoughts. She saw, with devastating clarity, that there was no getting the better of Juan Cregeen. Apart from looking her best she had meant the evening to be no different from any other spent with a young attractive man, but feelings were creeping in; first a sentimentality for Mr Kelly's wishes, and a kind of worry for herself in the dilemma she faced about it. And now to crown it all here was something much more alarming; something she had to tone down and escape from before...

The face she turned up to him belied the tumult inside her.

'Would you like a drink before we go?' she asked.

He shook his head. 'I'm no great drinker. When Richard has finished his we'll go.'

Richard emptied his glass and stood up, looking smaller in stature than he really was against the wide-shouldered, slim-hipped frame of Juan looking particularly handsome in evening dress.

Richard said, 'I'm ready when you are.'

His grey eyes twinkled and his smile included them both. Nora liked him, but it irritated her to see that he sensed a romance between her and Juan.

He could not be more wrong, she thought wryly.
It was a cue for her to keep her feelings in check,
to harden herself against Juan's undoubted charm.
After all, she was not the first girl to fall in love
with a man's physical attractions and she would not
be the last.

Tricia was the first person Nora saw as they entered a bar bordering on a sea of immaculately set
tables. She wore a red dress with a plunging neckline. Her companion was an elderly man and her
jewelled dangling earrings caught the light as she
smiled up at him.

Leaving Nora with Richard Garrant, Juan went
to the bar for drinks. Nora watched him speak to
the barman, then turn to speak to Tricia, saw
his easy smile as he spoke to her apparently in jest.
Was he in love with Tricia? Was he ... came the
irrepressible thought, and Nora hastily shrugged
off a subject which was better left alone.

It did occur to her, though, that Tricia was a
femme fatale who was out to find a husband again.
Aimée was an unhappy encumbrance and the poor
child was probably aware of the fact, which explained why she had wound herself into Juan's affections. Was Tricia playing on that and imprisoning
him in her toils too?

Finn Cullan strolled up to them as Juan returned
with the drinks, and complimented Nora on being
the prettiest girl in the room. The evening as far
as Nora was concerned was hardly a success. She had
plenty of partners during the dancing which followed, as did Tricia. Once when she was dancing
with Finn, Nora saw Juan pass with Tricia and his
expression as he looked down at her was one which
was unmistakably appreciative of her charms.

When the dance finished Juan strolled over with

Tricia to where Nora stood with Finn. With a gesture of his head he indicated a corner table not far from the bar seating four.

'I'll fetch refreshments,' he volunteered, 'if you'll sit down over there.'

Finn seated Nora and Tricia and hitching up immaculate trousers sat between them.

'Enjoying your stay on the island?' he asked Nora.

'Very much. No, thanks.' She shook her head as Finn offered a cigarette before turning to Tricia, who took one in scarlet-tipped fingers.

Tricia inhaled, blew out a line of smoke and gazed at Nora between heavily made up lashes.

'I've been told you've made a hit with Aimée,' she said. 'Normally she's very shy of making friends, but she likes you.'

'I like her too,' Nora answered sincerely. 'She's very sweet and unspoiled.'

Tricia glanced at Finn who was returning his lighter to his pocket after lighting his cigarette, then she said sweetly,

'I'm so grateful to Finn for asking us to spend a holiday with him, but I'm afraid Aimée is in danger of being completely spoiled. Everyone makes such a fuss of her. At home I try to be very casual with her. It's so easy to overdo the mother part. Actually what she needs is a father.'

'In short,' Finn cut in, 'you need a husband?' He eyed her thoughtfully. 'If you didn't make it so obvious you'd probably get one.'

Tricia laughed. 'That's a bit below the belt, I must say! Since we're speaking so frankly who do you suggest? Aimée is very fond of Juan.'

Finn looked thoughtfully at the tip of his cigarette. 'I hardly think you would marry to please the child. First you have to get your man, whoever he happens to be fond of.'

'Is that a challenge that I couldn't get Juan?' she asked with a strange light in her eyes which Nora swiftly lowered her own against.

Finn looked at her directly. 'I wouldn't think with one divorce behind you that you'd even contemplate the idea of a second one on those terms,' he said darkly.

Tricia laughed again, and shrugged pretty shoulders. 'I suppose a woman in my position has to take what she can get when a child of a previous marriage is involved.'

Nora said, 'Why didn't you let your husband have Aimée? Or didn't he want her?'

She was feeling profoundly sorry for the child, since it was obvious that Tricia resented the responsibility.

'He's the chivalrous kind, thinks a child is better off with its mother.'

Tricia's tones were as hard as the look in her eyes, but it was transformed by Juan approaching with a tray of drinks.

'Darling Juan,' she cooed, 'you're an angel! My throat is absolutely parched.'

'That comes of drinking more than is good for you,' he answered, putting the tray down on the table.

'How sweet of you to notice,' she cooed. 'I'm afraid no one is bothered about poor little me.'

'Why should they be?' Juan reasoned carelessly. 'Nature has been kind in handing all her choice bits to you.'

A wave of colour spread over Nora's face as she watched his long lean fingers pouring out drinks to the sound of the clinking of ice against glass. Evidently Juan was accustomed to taking in a woman's charms, although he had not seemed the type. That frivolous comment could put him in the same category as Tricia as far as Nora was concerned.

She sipped her drink, hoping it would infuse some warmth in her since she was feeling completely numb. Juan sat down between her and Finn and swallowed part of his drink.

Tricia's slim fingers with blood-red tips were curved around her drink while she flung back her head to exhale cigarette smoke above her.

'I missed you today, Juan,' she said. 'I went around the bay with Kevin, but I didn't enjoy it as much as when you take me. I was in the water more than I was on the skis. Kevin isn't very good at it.'

Juan was surveying her with a mocking intensity. 'Kevin is good at other things—and I'm sure you've discovered that by the way you were making eyes at him just now,' he drawled.

'I wasn't making eyes at him,' she snapped angrily. 'You're in a beastly mood this evening. If you've had a bad day don't take it out on poor little me!'

Juan smiled. 'As a matter of fact I've had a most enjoyable day with Nora.'

The last two words were murmured with a kind of subtle emphasis, and Nora felt her face go hot. She had no wish to join in any squabble and it seemed to her that Tricia was ripe for one.

'We've been to the Calf of Man,' she said quietly. 'Juan had some business in Port St Mary and offered to take me.'

'How nice!' Sarcasm dripped from Tricia's tones. 'Juan is good at picking naive girls up to show them the island, even little girls like my daughter. It's surprising how girls go for a uniform hat, especially a yachting one.'

'Stop it!' Juan spoke sternly. 'You know that isn't

true, and keep away from Kevin Stroud. He contaminates everything he touches. All he has is money.'

Tricia speared him with a venomous look. Furiously she blurted, 'I'd say that was enough to make him interesting. Besides, if you'd been around I wouldn't have gone with him.'

Juan was unperturbed. 'So what? I'm not here at anyone's beck and call—Finn will verify that.'

Finn, however, was remaining an amused spectator. He refused to be drawn, and if Tricia had not been so angry she would have taken notice of Juan's steely look.

'I don't know what's got into you, Juan,' she said. 'It wouldn't have anything to do with Nora inheriting a fortune, would it? Nice to have a bit on the side and money to boot.'

Juan said slowly, darkly, 'If you were a man I'd knock you down for that. What an unpleasant person you are! It's time somebody took you in hand.'

Tricia's smile was not pleasant. 'You know, that's funny, because I thought you had. You've captured Aimée's affections to the extent that she's been regarding you as a father figure ever since we came here.'

Juan said distastefully, 'I find this conversation in very bad taste—and you owe Nora an apology.'

'For what?' Tricia scoffed insolently.

Finn said quietly, 'I think you'd better apologise, Tricia. You were very rude and insulting, and I don't allow any guests of mine to insult my friends.'

Tricia looked mortified. 'O.K., if that's what you want, I apologise,' she snapped. 'Now, if you'll excuse me I'll move to more congenial company.'

She swept away without a backward glance and Nora saw her join Kevin Stroud at the bar. Music for dancing had started again and when Richard Garrant came to join them, Juan asked Nora if she would like to dance.

She followed him on to the dance floor wishing she had not agreed to come. She did not fit in with them at all. But, too soon, her whole being was by way of relenting with her resentment forming a kind of pain.

'Sorry about the incident just now,' said Juan above her ear. 'Tricia will have to watch it or her holiday will be cut short. Knowing Finn, she'll probably end up on a plane back home.'

'She's probably resenting me,' Nora suggested. 'After all, you were giving her more of your attention before I happened along. She lost her temper, that's all. It would be a pity if she had to go when Aimée is looking so much better.'

She felt his fingers curl around the hand he held, but she took care that her own did not respond. He danced well, as his congenital ease of movement indicated that he would, and he held her correctly.

But he was much too close for her to relax entirely. It was a situation which she was finding more impossible with every minute.

'Do you mind if I go after this dance?' she asked.

'Not at all. I'll come with you—I want to talk to you. We can either talk in your place or any place you choose,' he said easily.

Nora looked up at him. 'Talk?'

'Yes. We can find a corner here if you like where we shan't be overheard.'

She shook her head. 'No, we can go to the flat. But I don't know what we've got to talk about.'

Back in her flat Nora felt on home ground. There was a tranquillity about it which lulled her into thinking that nothing unpleasant could happen there.

'Sit down,' she said when they were in the small lounge. 'What would you like to drink?'

'Do we want a drink?' Juan queried on a dark uplifted brow.

'I'd like a coffee,' she confessed. 'What about you?'

'I'm easy,' he answered.

Nora made the coffee and imagined what it would be like married to Juan. She did not call in to him by way of conversation, for she could not think of a word to say. When their cups were filled with the fragrant liquid they still did not speak. It seemed that Juan, now that they were settled, seemed reluctant to begin their little talk.

At length he put down his cup and felt in his pocket for cigarettes.

'Mind if I smoke?' he asked after she shook her head as he offered them to her. 'I seem to be smoking more since I met you. I'll have to cut it out. I can if I want.'

'What have I to do with it?' she asked. 'I smoke very rarely myself.'

'You'd be surprised,' he answered, replacing the cigarettes and lighter to his pocket. 'Do you mind if I speak out?'

'Fire away,' she said lightly. 'This seems to be an evening for plain speaking.'

'You're sore at Tricia. Don't be. I have a way of preventing her from making any more snide remarks. This cousin of yours that you're in partnership with—do you like him a lot?'

'He's good company, easy to work with, but I don't think those are qualities enough for marriage. I don't love him, if that's what you mean,' she said frankly.

'Good. I suggested it to you before that we should

get together. Now it seems we both need to do this, especially me. You see, Tricia is a menace and one that I don't much like. She is serious about our relationship; I'm not. Not only that, she's proving an embarrassment to Finn as well. He's been kind enough to offer her a holiday here for the sake of Aimée and she saw it as an opportunity to get a husband. It didn't take her long to discover that Finn wasn't interested.'

'So she set her sights upon you,' put in Nora.

'In a way. I don't want her to play on Aimée's feelings by pretending that there's something betweeen us, that some day she might have a new daddy—me. The child is lonely and it would be wrong to build up her hopes.'

Nora considered this without raising her eyes to his face.

'I see what you mean,' she said slowly, talking to her coffee cup. 'How much longer is Tricia staying on the island? Is she here for the summer?'

'A month, maybe more. I might be gone before she goes.'

'When...when do you go?' Nora had never known a future that looked so bleak since she lost her parents.

Juan took a pull at his cigarette. Without much expression, he said, 'I'll let you know when the time comes. Meanwhile you and I can be seen around now and then together. We needn't make heavy weather of it. The word soon goes round when two people are seen enjoying each other's company.'

Nora lifted her face to meet his eyes. Speech evaded her for breathless seconds as he held her gaze. Then she said,

'I don't mind going out with you occasionally.'

'Thanks,' he said dryly. 'I'll let you off lightly. I might drop in some time.'

She nodded. 'I'd like that.'

He crushed out his cigarette in a nearby ashtray and rose to his feet. 'That's settled, then. Goodbye for now. Sleep well.'

CHAPTER SEVEN

DESPITE her worries Nora's sense of wellbeing increased enormously. She was asleep as soon as her head touched the pillow at night and she woke up every morning filled with the joys of being perfectly fit. Each morning now, weather permitting, she went for a swim in the sea or at the swimming pool on the promenade.

She had been for a swim in the sea, returned to the flat to dress and was going for her daily newspaper when she noticed the familiar big car parked not far from the newsagents in the shopping precinct. Juan strolled towards her as she left the shop.

'Good morning,' he greeted her with a grin. 'Did you have a lie-in this morning?'

'No. I've been for my early morning dip.'

Slowly his dark eyes moved from her bright hair to the clear brown eyes, and her glowing peach-bloom complexion. Her sundress, tiny pink polka dots on white cotton, was fresh and enchantingly revealed golden limbs.

'I can see what they mean about the early bird catching the worm,' he murmured, his eyebrows raised in appraisal. 'What enticing bait for any man who gets up in the morning! Meeting you on the beach is going to give them an appetite for something more than food.'

Nora's heart beat suffocatingly. It wasn't fair for vital and dangerously attractive young men like Juan Cregeen to take one unawares, she thought, deliberately steeling herself against his undoubted charm.

'Swimming gives one an appetite for food in my case,' she said demurely. 'So I'm sure you'll excuse me, since I have yet to have my breakfast.'

'Close your windows, won't you, while you're preparing it. I have yet to have mine.' He gave her a quizzical look. 'You could spare a cup of coffee? I won't go further than that. Bit early yet for coffee locally.'

Nora eyed him warily. 'Run out of coffee on the boat, have you?'

'The boat isn't there. It's gone in the local shipyard for repairs.'

'It was there when I went bathing.'

'So you did notice it?'

Again that infuriating eyebrow shot up and Nora could have kicked herself for her slip of the tongue.

'One becomes accustomed to seeing it there. It kind of blends in with the surroundings. Incidentally, it's company for me when I look out of my window at night.'

Her eyes shied away from probing dark eyes and the faint smile on the well-cut lips. Juan was not in sailing garb this morning. He was wearing superbly cut slacks in beige with a matching safari style jacket, and a brown silk shirt with a cravat tucked in at his firm brown throat. He wore no hat, and the crisp curling hair looked as strong and vibrant as the man himself.

'I didn't go to the boat last night. A workman from the shipyard towed it away this morning. About that coffee?'

Nora found herself resenting his assurance and he was surveying her with an enigmatic look which was maddening, to say the least.

Reluctantly she answered, 'So long as your appetite only concerns food, you're welcome to a coffee.'

He smiled and her heart lurched. Her sympathy

was for all the girls who adored the contrast of white teeth against a good-looking masculine face, and crisply curling hair accentuated by a yachting cap.

'The trouble is,' she told him, following him into the lounge of her flat, 'you make this place look cramped with your height and breadth of shoulder. Better sit down and read the newspaper while I get the breakfast. What do you say to a slice of succulent ham and two eggs?'

He grinned. 'My stomach is already answering for me! It's applauding without reservations. At least let me help.'

'Very well. You can fry the ham and eggs while I get the bread and butter for my boiled egg.'

Nora laid the table in a place reserved for eating at one end of the lounge, boiled her egg and filled plate with bread and butter. She gave Juan a slice of bread to fry along with the ham and eggs and placed a slice of melon beside his plate, another beside her own.

They sat down to the pleasing aroma of freshly made coffee. Nora's heart had thudded away during the preparation of the meal which continually brought her in close contact with Juan. Now she was seated opposite to him at the table, and she was not feeling very much at home with him. He made her feel elegant and cherished, like a teenager being entertained by Prince Charming. Furthermore, he had cooked his breakfast to an appetising golden brown.

'You're very self-sufficient, aren't you?' she remarked, spooning out the soft flesh of the melon. 'I couldn't have cooked it better myself.'

'Can you cook?' he asked mockingly. 'I know you can boil an egg—or can you?'

He looked darkly at the brown egg set in an eggcup near to her melon.

'Very funny,' she said witheringly. 'Allow me to demonstrate.'

Having finished the melon Nora tapped the top of her egg with a spoon, and looked challengingly at his twinkling eyes.

'I like the yolk to be soft but the white firm,' she said, and deftly took off the top of the egg. 'There! What do you think about that?'

Proudly she showed him the perfectly cooked egg.

He nodded. 'You can boil an egg,' he conceded.

'Thanks.' Her voice was filled with sarcasm. 'You'd be surprised what I can do.'

'I'll bear that in mind,' he said, eating with slow obvious enjoyment.

'Don't they feed you at Finn's place?' she asked sweetly, spooning up the golden yolk of her egg.

'I didn't have time for anything this morning. I left early. I'm taking Aimée to the Wild Life Park this afternoon. She wants you to come too.'

'What about Tricia? Isn't she going?'

Nora reached for a slice of bread and butter and avoided his eyes. She was trying to figure out why Juan should spend most of his time taking Aimée around. While he would never regard the girl's mother as a potential wife he appeared to be working quite close to some relationship between them.

Juan said softly, 'No, Tricia is not going.' He reached out for his coffee. 'One thing women have in common—they all need a man as a status symbol to spell security with the usual money bags. If their spouse has bags under the eyes through making his money they can ignore them by looking down at his cheque book.'

Nora heard herself saying casually, 'There are men who hunt the fleshpots as well, men who marry women for their money.'

'True,' murmured Juan coolly and agreeably. 'It's all in the game.'

'So you think Tricia is out for a husband?'

He shrugged, looked at her shrewdly as he put down his half empty cup.

'Not getting bored going out with us, are you?' he commented.

Nora gave a small laugh. 'Of course not! I want to go out and see more of the island, that's all.'

'The Wild Life Park is part of the island, and a very interesting part.'

She nodded. 'I know, but I just want to take it in my own time.'

'You mean you wouldn't enjoy it with Aimée and me?'

Nora gave a pained smile. 'You know I would, only I have the car and ...'

'You want to get on with it?' he picked her up sharply.

'Oh dear, I seem to have put my foot in it, don't I? I'd like to come with you.'

Juan said curtly, 'Come off the rack! You don't have to. Kids are very perceptive and Aimée would know right away whether you'd come with us because you want to.'

Nora coloured slightly. 'I'm never moody and I would never take anything out on a child. Furthermore, I'd planned on borrowing a book from the local library and taking a picnic out in the country.'

'So I'll tell Aimée you have another engagement and won't be able to come with us. Did you know that at home Aimée is left mostly in care of a neighbour? I thought it would have been a treat for her to go out for a change with a couple who would give her a taste of family life.'

Nora paused with the last spoonful of egg on its way to her mouth.

'But isn't that rather cruel, encouraging her in daydreams? I mean, she has to get used to being part of a one-parent family. That is, until her mother marries again.'

'Tricia loves her father. He takes her out once a month and she stays with him for that weekend.'

Nora popped the spoonful of egg into her mouth and met the worldly-wise expression on his tanned handsome face with the impression that he regarded her as denying an unhappy child a treat.

With more vigour than she intended she turned the eggshell bottom up in the eggcup and drove the point of her spoon through the centre of the shell.

'What did you do that for?' enquired Juan in soft jibing tones. 'Were you unconsciously stabbing at me?'

Nora answered honestly and frankly. 'No, I wasn't. You're supposed to make a wish. It was something my mother taught me as a child to encourage me to eat my egg. I still do it.'

'And does the wish come true?'

Her brown eyes met his dark ones disarmingly. 'Sometimes. I suppose you think it's childish? Well, a lot of childish things are fun.'

He said darkly, 'A lot of grown-up things can be fun too. Why not combine the two and enjoy an afternoon at the Wild Life Park with that intention?'

'I've said I'll come,' she reminded him.

'Good. I'll see that one or two childish games are thrown in for good measure,' he promised sardonically.

'More coffee?' Nora asked sweetly with the wicked feeling of wanting to drown him in it.

He proffered his cup and it did not need a glance at him to know that he was eyeing her with a faint mockery. He stayed to help her wash up, insisting upon doing his bit, as he put it, towards paying for his meal. They were bitter-sweet moments spent passing him the dishes to wipe, and the flat was very empty when he had gone.

When Juan picked her up early that afternoon his big car was empty.

'No Aimée?' she queried as he put her in the front seat beside him.

'We're calling for her. I had business which kept me on the go, ending with a lunch.'

'What exactly do you do?' Nora asked curiously.

'I would only bore you,' he answered, and swung the car up the small incline towards the promenade. Then he turned left and drove along the entrance to the quay where boats were unloading their cargo.

'Try me,' she said.

'I'll qualify that remark of mine by saying I would bore myself,' he drawled.

'I'm sure no man is ever bored talking about himself,' Nora commented.

Her uneasiness was wearing off. She felt the tangy salt air breezing in and lifting her golden locks— saw the harbour crammed now with yachts and a few fishing vessels and looked eagerly at the beautiful swans gliding in the vicinity of the swing bridge.

To her left, the picturesque row of shops, warehouses and cottages had not as yet fallen to the greed of the speculator who seemed bent on destroying the character of the island.

'I never tire of coming this way,' she smiled with sparkling eyes. 'The scenery is so beautiful you feel you want to put it down on canvas.' She sighed, and glanced at Juan. 'You were saying...'

He raised a dark brow. 'Ah yes. Yesterday I would have waxed eloquently about the business in hand because it was a challenge for me to succeed in what I set out to do. Now it's all over. Success is mine. Need I say more?'

Nora's throat felt a little tight. 'Does that apply to the women in your life as well? You lose all interest once you've achieved your aim?'

'Let's say I prefer the plums I can pick to the ones that fall into my lap. There's nothing that keeps the adrenalin going like going ahead to do your own thing.'

Nora said huskily, 'Would you say I fell into your lap like a ripe plum?'

They had wound their way in between cars and trucks to the end of the quay and Juan swept out on to the main road.

'I was under the impression that you'd fallen into the sea. I seem to remember taking you to the boat to dry off. However, my sweet one, don't try to analyse the workings of a man's mind. He's a wily animal.'

'You'd make a good politician. You know how to get round questions without answering them,' Nora told him tartly.

'I'll remember that,' he replied, unperturbed. 'I might need a job some day.'

The car was flashing along leafy roads of sunlight where tall trees met overhead in places and cottages were few and far between. Nora wished it was as restful in the car as outside it. For some reason she could never succeed in being free and easy with Juan. It might have been her imagination, but all his actions, his conversation, seemed aimed to get at her in some way. Did he always have to be so masculine, so forceful in her presence? She knew he was not that way with Aimée.

Aimée was waiting for them at the gates of the Armitage with an enormous teddy bear in her arms.

'Goodness,' Nora exclaimed, 'Is she bringing that toy with her?'

Juan grinned. 'There's room enough for them both on the back seat. She obviously wants you to see it.'

Aimée did. 'Look what Juan bought me,' she cried with delight as he opened the car door to put her and the toy into the back seat. 'Isn't he beautiful?'

'Very,' agreed Nora. 'He has a nice face and he's cuddly.'

'That's why I chose him. Juan liked this one too —didn't you, Juan?'

Aimée gazed at Juan adoringly as he moved round to slide into the driving seat. He grinned as he surveyed them both before starting the car.

'It was a toss-up between the teddy and a gorilla. The teddy won,' he said.

The outsize teddy was left in the car while they went in the Wild Life Park. Aimée enjoyed it and they had tea while watching the flamingoes and swans on the lake. Throughout the afternoon Juan had patiently explained and pointed out things of interest to Aimée, with one or two mocking glances in Nora's direction.

Where Nora was concerned the presence of Aimée had helped considerably in her attitude towards Juan. She had not addressed him much but there had been times when she had felt him watching her speculatively.

They were returning to the car when Aimée said, 'Can we go to your flat, Nora, please? Mummy will be out when I get back and I shall go to bed early.'

Nora meditated. 'Perhaps Mummy won't like you staying out, dear,' she said, avoiding Juan's gaze.

Aimée said eagerly, 'Mummy won't mind. She didn't care if I stayed with friends or not back home. Mrs Shipley next door says I'm more part of her family than her own children. Please, Nora, let me stay! I'm enjoying my holiday so much.'

Juan put in glibly, 'Maybe Nora has other plans for this evening. Could be some Prince Charming is coming to take her out.'

'Is he?' Aimée asked with round eyes.

'No,' replied Nora. After a long moment she added, 'Stay if you want.'

'Oh, thank you!' Aimée hugged Nora before getting into the car.

At the flat the child was enchanted with the guest bedroom, which Nora told her she was the first to occupy. All three set in to prepare the meal for the evening and there was much laughter and jostling in the small kitchen.

Jony called unexpectedly and stared nonplussed at the domestic scene. Aimée had a tea-towel pinned around her waist and a smut of flour on her nose, while Juan was cleaning the vegetables.

Nora greeted him warmly, sensing his embarrassment. 'Hello, Jony,' she smiled. 'I don't believe you've met Aimée, a friend of mine. I think you know Juan?'

The two men acknowledged each other with a brief nod.

Jony came right to the reason for his visit. 'I thought you might like to come to have a meal at the farm this evening, but I can see it's not convenient,' he said awkwardly, refusing to sit down.

'I'm sorry,' Nora's smile was apologetic. 'Some other time, perhaps. I'd love to come.'

When he had gone, she said, 'I ought to have asked him to stay for supper. After all, there's plenty. I could have opened a bigger tin of tongue to go with the salad and there's practically a whole chicken since I only had a small portion of it last evening.'

'Stop dithering,' cut in Juan. 'The man would

have been too embarrassed to stay. He probably had everything planned for you tonight, right down to the flowers and candles on the table.'

Nora sliced hardboiled eggs up for the salad with unnecessary force.

'What if he had?' she cried indignantly. 'The thought was there.'

There was a short silence while she lifted her eyes from her task to encounter Aimée's apprehensive stare and Juan's uplifted eyebrows. Then her sense of humour bubbled to the surface.

'There goes my Prince Charming for the evening supper by candlelight and all,' she gurgled.

But Aimée was upset. 'I've spoiled your evening,' she wailed.

'Of course you haven't,' Nora told her firmly. 'We can have candles too, and I can always go another night to dine at the farm.'

Aimée brightened. 'So you can. Juan can be your Prince Charming for this evening too. I'll lend him to you—only lend, mind.'

Nora laughed. 'Thank you very much. I'm sure Juan will be delighted.'

Tomfoolery followed as Juan made a point of kissing Nora's hand before he seated her at the table. Jony unwittingly had made the evening a success and it was a very happy Aimée who went to bed in the pretty guest room with white bedroom furniture, offwhite rug and pretty lampshades and curtains.

Juan went to tuck her in with the enormous teddy bear. She had wilted long before the end of the meal and was almost fast asleep before he tucked her in.

Nora had put out the candles and opened the curtains when Juan returned to the lounge to the pleasant aroma of freshly made coffee. It was still daylight and the dying sun filled the room with a golden glow.

Juan lifted a brow at the change of scene, and Nora felt the colour rush under her clear skin.

There was outright amusement in his face as he said,

'Playing safe?'

He came forward with loose-jointed ease and flung himself on to the settee. Nora looked apprehensively at the vacant place beside him and murmured almost to herself,

'Hadn't you better telephone The Armitage to tell them that Aimée is spending the night here?'

His presence without the reassuring presence of Aimée was having a disastrous effect on her composure, but Juan could not have looked less concerned.

'Plenty of time, and stop dithering. Relax. Shall I pour the coffee?'

His tones were lazy as if he was thoroughly at home in his surroundings—which was more than could be said of Nora, whose heart was beating twenty to the dozen. To her surprise she poured out the coffee with a steady hand, gave him a cup and placed the low table between them as she took one of the chairs to sit in.

'Well, did you enjoy your visit to the Wild Life Park?'

Juan regarded her lazily over the rim of his coffee cup and Nora borrowed his coolness.

'Very much. I'm glad Aimée did. She doesn't have too good a time at home by all accounts. Where is Tricia, by the way? Aimée didn't expect her home early.'

'Helping out at the Yacht Club. Tricia prefers masculine company. I . . .' He stopped talking to listen.

Nora had heard something too. 'I'll go to see if Aimée is awake. I thought I heard her,' she said.

Aimée was lying in crumpled bedclothes as if she had been tossing and turning. She was lying on her stomach and her shoulders were heaving with muffled sobs.

'Aimée!' Nora cried in concern as she sat on the bed to turn her face upwards. 'What is it, darling?'

'I've got toothache and it's terrible,' the child gulped on a dry sob, her face blotched with crying. 'It woke me up.'

Nora pushed back the silky hair from her hot forehead and gathered her in her arms.

'Poor darling! What do you usually have for it? Is it a bad tooth?'

'I don't know. I've never had toothache before. It's horrible!'

'What's horrible?'

Juan was leaning against the door frame and Nora looked at him in distress.

'Aimée has toothache.'

He came to the bed and bent over her as Nora let Aimée sit up out of her arms.

'Open your mouth, honey,' he said gently. 'Tell me where the pain is.'

Aimée put a forefinger in her mouth and indicated the tooth in question.

'It looks healthy enough,' said Juan, peering into her mouth. 'Probably caught cold in it, my sweet.' He straightened and consulted his watch thoughtfully. 'Too late to get the doctor, but it's possible that Jony's girl, Cissy, could be calling on her friend along the corridor here. Being a nurse she might be able to suggest something. I'll see if I can find her.'

Nora gathered the convulsive little form against her and whispered words of comfort. It seemed ages before Juan was back with a young woman whom he introduced as Cissy Melly. Nora smiled warmly at an attractive young woman in her late twenties with small neat features and pretty grey eyes.

Leaving Juan with Aimée, they went to the kitchen to heat some milk. Cissy watched Nora pour milk into a pan.

'The only thing I can suggest,' she said, 'is part of a sleeping pill I've borrowed from my friend here. She takes one most nights. Taken in warm milk it could send her to sleep. If Aimée has caught cold in the tooth then the warm bed should do the rest.'

Aimée settled down at last, clinging to Juan's hand while Nora went to see Cissy out. Nora liked what she saw as a sweet and gentle person and decided that Jony was a fool not to marry her.

'We're very grateful for your help,' she said. 'Thanks.'

'Glad I could help,' Cissy smiled warmly. 'You're the girl who shares Jed Kelly's will with Jony, aren't you? I'm glad I've been able to make your acquaintance.' Cissy hesitated as if wondering whether to go on, then she plunged. 'I hope you won't think it cheek if I say that I hope you do marry someone in order to get your part of the money. You see, Jony will have enough as it is. I wouldn't want him to have twice as much as he'll have if he gets it all.'

Nora laughed. 'That's the last thing I expected you to say,' she admitted.

Cissy shrugged neatly clad shoulders. 'Too much money is not good for any one person. Jony has the farm, and the money he inherits will be more than enough, providing he has only his fair share. But don't tell him I said so, will you?'

'No, I won't,' Nora promised. 'I'll think about

it. Perhaps we can meet again some time soon.'

'I'd like that,' said Cissy.

When Cissy had gone Nora washed the dishes. She was taking the coffee cups from the lounge into the kitchen when Juan came in quietly.

'Let me take them. I'll help you wash up. Aimée is asleep, but I think I'll stay with her in case she wakes again during the night,' he said, following her into the kitchen.

'Do you think she will?'

'She might.'

He reached up over her head for the tea-towel and kissed her hair. Unconsciously, Nora stiffened.

'What was that in aid of?' she asked, moving away from him on the pretext of making room for more dishes on the drainer.

'An apology, if you like, for not taking Aimée home. She would have been better there. Finn's housekeeper would have taken it all in her stride.'

'But Aimée would have been just as upset if Tricia hadn't been there, surely?' Nora argued. 'I'm assuming that you wouldn't have been there either?'

'True,' he conceded. 'You like children, don't you?'

'Of course I do. I hope to have some of my own some day. The trouble with Aimée is that she needs a masculine shoulder to cry on—her father's.'

The dishes finished, Nora dried her hands and Juan, his task completed, watched her put cream on her hands.

'You aren't upset about me staying the night, are you?' he asked.

A wave of colour swept over her face. He was standing too close. Minus his jacket, his shoulders had a military squareness in the well tailored shirt. He looked big and uncaring.

Nora massaged her hands and tried to borrow some of his coolness.

'No, I'm grateful in a way. I only hope Aimée has a good night.' Nora kept her head lowered against his probing gaze. 'I'll be grateful if you stay.'

Juan took her arm lightly and led her to a chair in the lounge. Then he drew the curtains, shutting them into a world of their own.

'What did you think of Cissy?' he asked, taking the other chair not far away.

'I liked her. She's quite nice really.'

He thrust out long legs as if settling down for the night.

'Yes, she is,' he confirmed. 'Tell you anything, did she?'

She nodded. 'Enough to know that she's a sensible person.'

The corner of his well-cut mouth quirked a little.

'Define sensible. I fail to see much sense in hanging around someone for ten years without a hint of matrimony.'

'Perhaps Cissy knows what she wants and is prepared to wait until she gets it,' she retorted with a hint of antagonism. 'She has sense enough to know that too much money can spoil a person.'

'Depends upon the person, doesn't it?' he replied coolly. 'I know plenty of people that wealth hasn't spoiled. Does that mean she's in favour of you marrying and so carrying out the terms of the will in order to get your share of the estate?'

Nora said philosophically, 'That's the general idea.'

'Set you thinking, has it?' mockingly.

'I've never stopped thinking about it. It isn't anything one can decide in a hurry.'

He grinned. 'You could put an ad in the local

paper saying "Bridegroom needed for a short space of time".'

Nora felt her nerves tighten at his careless attitude. She moistened dry lips. 'It's an idea. Why didn't I think of that?'

'You probably would eventually. Very dicey, though. You'd have to make it all legal by drawing up a document for him to sign in order to keep him within bounds. After all, there'd be two glittering prizes, your charming self and the money.'

By now Nora's feelings, already bruised by his mockery, were bordering on acute indignation. 'Are you in the legal profession?' she demanded.

'No, I'm not.' He was amused by her sudden wary expression. 'But two heads are always better than one in solving problems.'

Nora stifled a yawn. Night time, especially with a disturbing presence in the room, was no time for discussing problems, however urgent.

Juan heaved himself out of the comfortable chair. 'I'll look in to see if Aimée is still asleep,' he said in a low voice.

Somehow Nora had the impression that he was of the same opinion regarding problems at night. It was vexing, though, that the one friend she felt she could trust happened to be so uncaring about her predicament. She did hope, though, that poor Aimée would have a good night.

Juan came back with a smile of satisfaction. 'Fast asleep,' he said. 'I'll sit up with her in case I fall asleep in the lounge and don't hear her. She won't make a fuss. Aimée's a good little trouper. She probably won't waken until morning. It might be a punctured tooth, but it could be a shortage of calcium.'

Nora's sense of humour got the better of her. She had to laugh at his arrogance.

On a quiet ripple of mirth, she gurgled, 'You'd make an excellent father. How's the paternal instinct?'

Narrow-eyed, he looked down at her darkly.

'Is that an invitation to start a family?' he queried. 'Or are you being precocious?'

Nora sobered to stare up at him with bright alarmed eyes. But he did not wait for her to speak. He bent down to draw her out of her chair.

'You'd better go to bed,' he said grimly.

'Yes, I had.' His arms had dropped and she turned away. 'If you have no objection,' she answered.

'None whatever.' Moments ticked by as he looked down at the golden hair forming a halo around her face under the light. She looked young and defenceless, as vulnerable as Aimée. There was something else too—she was scared of him.

He bent his head and his fingers gripped the upper part of her arms. His kiss bruised, forcing back her head. Nora was in no position to understand that he was showing his resentment at her lack of trust in him. It was like teetering on the brink of a furnace with her body being scorched by the heat. She closed her eyes. A kind of bliss churned inside her, followed by a flaring need.

He let her go as suddenly as he had taken her, glaring down at her with hard glittering eyes.

'That's what you're afraid of, isn't it?' The kind of preliminaries leading to actual lovemaking. Only it isn't anything like that.' He drew a deep exasperating breath. 'Let's regard it as a goodnight kiss from Prince Charming. It might not be twelve o'clock, but this prince is taking himself off. I'll be in Aimée's room, so you can forget I'm here. Goodnight.'

Nora was still gasping when she heard him close the door of the guest room. It seemed incredible to the point of fantasy that Juan should behave the way he had. What he had done was completely out of character. Yet was it not a fact that in thinking along such lines she had proved how little she really knew him?

She hardly knew what she was doing as she prepared for bed. Had the fire and need experienced in his arms been an illusion brought on by his manly charms? Was that the reason the flat changed its personality when he was there? One thing was for certain: she was not the same Nora Bain who had come to the island so lightheartedly.

That person had not known the sharp stab of desire, the hunger of need for someone who could not have cared less.

CHAPTER EIGHT

THE instant Nora awoke memory came flooding back. Those moments in Juan's arms, despite the rough handling, had been bitter-sweet and spiced with danger. This morning she had to face him as if nothing had happened, and she dreaded it. Her watch said nine o'clock. She had overslept.

She had one leg out of bed to get up when Aimée came in fully dressed and carrying a cup of tea.

Brightly she chirped, 'I've been up ages. Juan said to let you sleep. He went out to fetch his shaving things.' She giggled. 'He rubbed his chin around my face when I awoke this morning. It was rough and funny.'

Nora pushed herself up in bed and accepted the tea. 'How is the toothache?' she queried.

Aimée sighed with blissful inconsequence. 'It's gone.' She sat on the bed and whispered conspiratorially, 'Do you know what? Juan sat up with me all night in case I woke up with toothache. Wasn't he kind? He pulled all kind of faces when he woke up in the chair. He is funny. He's getting breakfast.'

With the inconsequential nonchalance of the young Aimée chatted on while waiting for Nora to drink her tea. If only I could be as free and easy with Juan as Aimée is, Nora thought dismally. It was going to be very difficult meeting Juan again without embarrassment after what had happened. But it had to be done.

The morning was sunny and promising. Nora washed and dressed quickly, put on a sun dress in primrose and white and went along the small corridor to the lounge where breakfast was already laid on the table.

'Good morning. Sleep well?' Juan's brows went up accompanied by a charming smile.

Evidently he had already forgotten about last night as he pulled out her chair.

'I overslept,' she confessed. 'I hope you did?' She laughed. 'Had a good night, I mean.'

That small laugh seemed to clear the air, and Nora found herself staring down at the slice of melon and brown boiled egg set in front of her.

Juan had sat down to watch her reaction with a trace of the old mockery glinting beneath his smile.

'I trust the egg is done to your liking,' he said, his regard steady and tantalising.

He was wearing a silk knit white sweater with a polo neck. Against it his face was mahogany brown, his teeth startlingly white.

Aimée was munching toast. 'Juan has brought your morning paper,' she said.

Nora glanced at the folded newspaper near to her elbow on the table, and murmured her thanks. Her egg was done exactly how she liked it. When the top had been taken off she looked up to see Juan watching her. He seemed to have his tongue in his cheek.

'Cooked to perfection,' she said.

'Glad you like it,' he said lazily.

Aimée did most of the talking, and they left soon after breakfast.

When Aimée went into the bedroom for her out-size teddy bear, Juan said in an undertone, 'I apologise for last night. I was angry with you. I shouldn't have been, because you gave us unstinted hospitality. Aimée is over the moon because she's stayed in your flat. She'll talk about it for days.'

Nora's clear eyes met his disarmingly. 'That's all right. I'm glad she enjoyed herself,' she answered frankly.

He pushed his hands into his pockets and surveyed her enigmatically.

'We are friends, aren't we?' he asked.

Before Nora could answer Aimée returned carrying the teddy bear. Nora still did not answer—whether because Aimée was there or some more subtle inference from Juan's manner and words she could not have said.

Juan spoke again. 'Be seeing you. Thanks for having us, and to Aimée, 'Thank Nora before we go.'

Aimée pushed the teddy bear into Juan's arms and grabbed Nora to kiss her soundly.

'Thank you, Nora. You will be coming to my birthday party on Saturday, won't you?'

Nora nodded, avoiding Juan's eyes. She said goodbye and closed the door of her flat with mixed feelings. It was fantastic to her way of thinking that Juan Cregeen should become an issue during her short stay on the island. But there it was. In some subtle fashion the magnetism of his personality lingered on, permeating the whole flat. Such was the power of his personality that it was impossible to dismiss him from her thoughts and Nora knew that he would continue to dominate her life while she was there.

It did not help to know that she had promised Aimée to go to her birthday party. But she could not disappoint the child. Nevertheless it would bring her in contact with Juan.

On Saturday morning Nora went for a swim, had a leisurely breakfast, then visited the supermarket in the shopping precinct. Juan was calling for her after lunch to take her to Aimée's birthday party, and he telephoned while she was having breakfast to remind her what day it was. The sound of his deep voice on the telephone set her nerves on edge and she was unable to concentrate fully on what she was doing.

Nora was quivering when she dressed after lunch, but her reflected image calmed her somewhat. The sun-dress with its wide skirt and trim nipped-in waist showed off her apricot tan to perfection. The matching little jacket in brown paisley cotton against a white background brought out the brown in her eyes.

But the composure she built up collapsed like a pack of cards when she met Juan. He seemed to be taller than ever and his white smile more mocking.

He said, 'Nice to find you ready and waiting, and so enchantingly sweet.'

Nora wished futilely that she could forget that kiss he had given her as easily as he appeared to. Or had he forgotten? The glint in his eyes told her nothing.

'There was no reason why you should call for me,' she told him perversely. 'I could have gone in my own car. The trouble is that you have to wait until the person who takes you is inclined to bring you back.'

He nodded. 'And that worries you, does it? Or are you worried about going with me because you aren't quite sure what to expect?'

He opened the car door as he spoke and waited for her to get in. If he was annoyed he did not show it but stood there with the infuriating nonchalance of a man who did not care what she felt or thought. Nora bit hard on her lip. Just keep like that, she thought, tantalising and uncaring. It will keep me on my mettle.

Aloud, she said firmly, 'Am I the only person you're picking up?'

His eyes narrowed. 'Were you hoping that there would be others?' He took the parcels containing presents for Aimée from her arms and put them on the back seat. 'Hop in,' he commanded curtly.

He bent down to push her skirt clear of the car door, then went round to the driving seat. Soon they were making for the open country. The loveliness of the tree-shaded roads and the fresh breeze blowing in warmly through the half open window lifted her spirits.

'How is Aimée?' she asked lightly. 'No more toothache, I hope?'

'No.' He took a swift sideways glance at her glowing cheeks, and the delicate skin at her temples revealed by her hair lifting in the breeze. 'For a lass with a delicate air you can be quite militant,' he added with a candid grin.

Her heart gave its familiar twist. As she smiled at him an unexpected sweet breath of air sent the golden hair across her eyes. Nora brushed it aside with pearl-tipped fingers.

'What's wrong with having a mind of your own?' she demanded sweetly.

'Nothing,' he replied with a smile in his voice. 'The last time I saw you I asked you a question which you didn't answer. Are we friends?'

'Of course we are. How many are coming to the party?'

'A dozen children with as many helpers. The number has to be equal these days if the house has to be kept standing.' He flashed a grin at her. 'I hope you're prepared for a rough and tumble? Aimée has to be protected a bit until she's stronger. Mind you, she's rather like you in a way. Her delicate appearance can be deceptive.'

'That's how girls should look. Feminine, just as you look big and protective.'

'Is that how I appear to you?' he jibed.

'It's how I hope you will be,' she corrected.

Juan said thoughtfully, dangerously, 'Now you have me wondering just how far is meant by protective?'

Involuntarily she laughed, and relaxed. 'Now you're teasing.' A pause. 'I suppose Tricia will be helping?'

'Sure. Finn has done most of the preparing, as you'll see. He was talking about roping in the kids from the orphanage.'

Nora saw what Juan meant when they arrived at the Armitage. A marquee had been erected upon the back lawn for the birthday tea. Children and some helpers were already gathered there when she arrived with Juan. Tricia gave her a careless nod which Aimée more than made up for by her rapturous welcome. Nora's birthday gifts were taken inside the house to be opened later and the fun began.

There were games and a puppet theatre and by the time tea was ready the fun was fast and furious. Everyone, children and grown-ups alike, sank gratefully into their chairs. Juan had worked harder than most. He had been indefatigable.

It was much later when the party was over and the children had gone that dinner that evening got under way. Aimée was given the place of honour at the head of the table with Finn.

No one had changed into evening dress. Because of Aimée the well-fitted bar at the end of the lounge had been left unlit. They had all sat down in the luxurious dining area to a champagne dinner. Aimée was allowed a small glass and she stood up to shyly voice her thanks to Finn and to all the helpers.

She ended on a wistful note, 'This is the first birthday I've had without Daddy, but Juan has been great. He stayed all night at Nora's flat when I had toothache, and rubbed his rough chin round my face like Daddy used to do to wake me the next morning.' She wrinkled her nose as she glanced at Juan seated not far away down the glittering table. 'He kisses nicely too—not grown-up kisses though like the ones he gives to Nora, but kind of Daddy kisses.'

The silence which followed the naïve little speech was lost on Aimée, who sat down quite unaware of having dropped a bombshell. The vicar and his wife looked shattered and Nora did not know what to do with her face. She looked across the table at Juan, who had flushed beneath his tan.

Finn had his tongue in his cheek, but Tricia was the furious one.

'Well, well!' she exclaimed. 'You shouldn't tell tales out of school, Aimée. I'm sure you're making it up.'

'Why should she make it up? It was all perfectly above board,' Juan put in lazily without turning a hair. 'May I present Mrs Juan Cregeen?'

Nora broke out in a cold sweat as he stood up and gestured to her to do the same. There was a strained silence while she rose on trembling legs with her nails digging into the palms of her hands. Everyone said congratulations, except Tricia, who looked strangely white.

'And to think that my own daughter knew and never told me!' she exclaimed.

Aimée said, 'But it isn't for keeps, Mummy. I only lent Juan to Nora until I grow up. Then I'm going to marry him.'

Everyone laughed at this bit of childish logic and

a toast for the happy couple was called for. Not long after Aimée was sent to bed and Tricia went up with her. But she was soon down again, asking Juan to go up in her place.

'You're a fast worker, I must say,' Tricia caught up with Nora when everyone left the dining table to seek the comfortable chairs in the lounge. 'Nothing Aimée said made sense, but what you've done does. I suppose it's all to do with the will. I didn't think you had it in you. It just goes to show it never pays to go by appearances.'

'I suppose it came as a bit of a shock,' Nora said almost apologetically. She almost admitted that it was a shock to herself to find she was married to Juan without a ceremony.

He had acted like the gentleman he was to shield her from gossip. But where did they go from here? In that moment Nora bitterly regretted coming to the birthday party.

She told Juan so when he was driving her back to the flat.

'Why take that attitude?' he said reasonably. 'Now admit that this whole thing about the will of a senile old man has been getting you down.'

'Mr Kelly was not senile!' she began hotly, then simmered down. 'There's something in what you say, but why add to my troubles by saying we're married?'

'It's a way out for you—a temporary marriage. With a husband behind you things will start moving. Why, Richard Garrant, your lawyer, was over the moon this evening when he congratulated us. He's delighted that he can clear the matter up instead of having it on his hands.'

Nora bit her lip. She said unhappily, 'Pretending that we're interested in each other and being married are two very different things. Besides, how do we get married without anyone knowing about it?'

'Easy enough. I know someone who'll do it for us. After all, you have your birth certificate here and all the necessary information. I can get the necessary forms and the proprietary legalities can be got through very quickly.'

'You make it sound so easy, as if you've planned it all out long ago.'

He said sardonically, 'My brain can work quickly in an emergency. Besides, I've found that some troubles have a way of working to a satisfactory solution on their own. This could be one of them.'

Nora tried to convince herself that this could be true, but only half-heartedly.

'I hope you're right,' she said wearily.

Preoccupied with her unhappy thoughts, she was only dimly aware of arriving at the entrance door to her flat. Coming to herself with a jerk, she turned to face Juan in the muted light of the car. Her face was white and strained.

'I'm grateful to you for what you've done, since it's as distasteful to you as it is for me. You had no other option. About tonight...' She broke off nervously.

'You mean our supposed married state?' He raised a dark brow. 'Nothing to worry about. I shall sleep on the boat. We're in the yacht race tomorrow morning and we return at ten o'clock tomorrow evening. On Monday I shall go to Douglas to collect the necessary forms for our marriage. Once the legal requirements have been gone through we can tie the knot.'

He spoke so calmly, as if he was discussing some business arrangement, while Nora had the sensation of being on the edge of something very dangerous and alarming.

She said quiveringly, 'I could go home. That would be the easy way out, wouldn't it?'

There was a short silence while he gave her a searching look. 'The coward's way out,' he mocked, and lifted a hand as she was about to speak. 'Just a moment. You seem to have the wrong impression. You must understand that it's a formality, a contract between two people that can be broken at any time.'

She sighed as if not entirely convinced. 'Shall you want me to go with you on Monday for the marriage forms?'

'It's a good idea if you do, taking your birth certificate and other documents.' He smiled. 'If anyone had told me a week ago that I'd be going on the yacht race a doomed man I would have said that they were round the bend!'

'But you've just said there's nothing to it?'

'There isn't. Oh, come on, smile! You haven't been really happy since you came here, have you?'

Curious and slightly incredulous, Nora stared at him. 'How do you know?'

He lifted wide shoulders. 'When you're not restless, you're on the defensive and you don't smile much. I refuse to believe it's the real you.' He placed an arm around her shoulders. 'Just think—when it's all cleared up you can have a good time with no worries, knowing you've done the right thing by Jed Kelly.'

He put his tanned cheek against her soft one and Nora just ached to enjoy the sanctuary of his arms. But he was comforting her as he would Aimée.

'I suppose I'm tired,' she said, moving out of his hold. 'It's been quite a day.'

With a murmured goodnight, she opened the

door of the car, slid out and went swiftly to the flat entrance. I'm in love with the man, and he hasn't the least idea of it, she thought despondently. I'm just another Aimée to him, someone who arouses his chivalry, someone he has to look after.

The yacht race began the next morning from the entrance to the harbour at the stone pier. Nora was up early, but she did not go to see it. It was a most peculiar morning, and she was alternating between breathless anticipation and fear. In one moment she fully decided to confess her love for Juan; in the next she shrank from seeing the dismay in his dark eyes. He would be utterly confounded, but he would deal with it in his chivalrous fashion, might even pretend that he returned her love just to spare her feelings.

Nora cringed at the thought. Somehow she had to get through the day without too many torturing thoughts. It was perfect weather for the yacht race, the sea as smooth as a millpond.

Around eleven Jony called. Nora would have welcomed a visit from anyone to take her mind off her troubles. Jony, covertly watchful at her cordial greeting sat down awkwardly in a chair, refusing her offer of coffee or a drink.

'I hear you've married Juan Cregeen,' he remarked.

'Goodness!' she cried. 'You know already? We...we didn't tell anyone until last night. Who told you?'

He shrugged heavy shoulders. 'Word gets around. This puts a new light on things.'

Nora perched on the arm of the chair opposite. 'I suppose it does.'

'You'll have to let the lawyer know.'

'He knows already. He was there at the time Juan announced it.'

'Clever of him. Though I'm not surprised. I knew he wouldn't let the grass grow under his feet. His kind never do.'

Steadily, Nora said, 'I don't think you have any reasons for saying that other than that he's attractive and also popular among his friends. You aren't jealous of him, are you? I don't mean where I'm concerned but for what he is.'

'Why should I be jealous? I've never had any time for his sort. A playboy, that's what he is. You might know you present a tempting proposition with what you stand to gain by marrying a Manxman.'

'I know that,' she returned. 'But I resent your remarks about Juan being a playboy.'

'Well he is, isn't he?' he insisted. 'Has he told you what he does for a living?'

'No, he hasn't.'

Jony's laugh lacked mirth. 'And you married him knowing nothing about him. You must be crazy, unless... was it the money?'

Nora's face deepened in colour. She said frigidly, 'I'm sorry. You must be very disappointed at not getting the entire estate, but it was what Mr Kelly wanted.'

'Maybe,' Jony conceded gruffly. 'Goes to show what people will do for money.'

Nora said sweetly, 'I suppose if the boot had been on the other foot it would have been all right for you to marry a Manx girl in order to qualify— a pity it wasn't. I don't think she would have much of a bargain, though, if it was Cissy, do you?'

He scowled fiercely. 'And what do you mean by that?'

'Well, you've kept her hanging about for ten years. Who do you think you are anyway? Cissy is very attractive and a nice person too. Juan likes her and there'll be many more who do. For all you know this might be your unlucky period. They say bad luck comes in threes.'

Jony stared at her blankly. 'How did you know I've just lost one of my cows?' he blurted.

Nora laughed, then apologised immediately. 'Oh, I'm sorry. But you know how news travels. I would say a good wife such as Cissy would make is far above the price of a cow or the money you'll lose by my marriage to Juan.'

Nora actually found she was enjoying herself. It did not matter that she had deceived him, that she had no idea that one of his cows had died. What mattered was that he would now get around to marrying Cissy, with a bit of luck.

She added for extra measure, 'You won't always have your housekeeper, you know.'

By now Jony's consternation had turned to anger. 'You've been spying on me, haven't you? You know about my housekeeper talking of going across the water to live with her sister?'

Nora stared wide-eyed at this disclosure. 'I had no idea she was thinking of leaving the island,' she told him frankly. 'But if this is true then I advise you to ask Cissy to marry you before she hears of it. Every girl has her pride, and she won't take kindly to being married just for convenience on your part.'

He rubbed his chin thoughtfully. 'Maybe it's time I settled down. I could do much worse, I reckon.'

'Worse?' Nora echoed indignantly. 'You'd be marrying a nurse, man, who could save you pounds in prescriptions with her knowledge of the sick.'

'You aren't so dumb, are you?' Jony smiled for the first time since arriving. 'I'll think about it.'

'You do that. Did you call just to see if it was

true about my marriage? Or was there something else?'

He was offended. 'It does concern me, you know. You've certainly kept it dark. Why didn't you let me know?'

'Because I didn't know myself...' Nora bit on her lip, blessing her unwary tongue. 'I mean, we made up our minds very quickly.'

'Is that why you're not wearing a wedding ring? Or did you put it away to keep the marriage secret?'

She said coolly, 'I'll be wearing it when I see you again. I see now that it's impossible to keep secrets here. I hope you aren't too disappointed about my marrying Juan?'

He shrugged his shoulders philosophically. 'Too late for that now. It was a crazy will in any case. I suppose you'll be going along the pier this evening to meet the conquering hero when he arrives?'

Nora felt her limbs stiffen. She went pale. 'I don't think so.'

Jony seemed surprised. 'Being the good little wife, are you, and cooking him a hot meal for when he returns?'

'I never thought of that,' she admitted weakly. 'I forgot it was Sunday. Thanks for reminding me.' She paused, wishing it was possible to read his thoughts. She had never got very close to Jony because he was the kind who would always keep one guessing. But there was more to it than that. The incident on the pier was something she would never forget, and now here he was wanting to know if she was going along that night.

Was there a motive behind his probing, his whole visit? Nora told herself not to be a fool. After all, there would be no motive in him wanting to harm her since she was married and the money she stood

to inherit would now go to Juan if anything did
happen to her.

All the same she said warily, 'Why did you ask if
I was meeting Juan on the pier this evening?'

Jony looked a little sheepish, went a dull red and
moved uneasily in his chair.

'Well, you being newly wed and all that,' he
mumbled.

Nora's fears fell away as she watched his embarrassment. She laughed with relief.

'You're blushing, Jony,' she cried accusingly. 'So
you are a bit romantic, after all?'

'I don't know about that,' he replied, getting
redder in the face. 'But being a farmer I know all
about the birds and the bees.'

It was Nora's turn to blush. 'I won't be going to
meet Juan, but I will cook a meal for when he returns.'

But as it turned out, she did go to meet Juan. She
was putting the finishing touches to the special
dinner she had prepared when she had a visitor.
Tricia came in wearing a short fur jacket over
slacks.

'I thought you'd like to go along the pier to meet
Juan,' she said by way of introduction. Her eyes
brightened at the pleasant aroma of cooking filling
the flat. 'Mmm, something smells nice.'

Nora watched her drop into a chair and loosen
the fur jacket. For the second time that day she was
trying to work out the motives of a caller. Maybe
she was becoming hypersensitive, or perhaps it was
because it was nearing ten o'clock and time for
Juan's return.

'Nice little place you have here.' Tricia gazed
around the lounge with approval. 'When the curtains are drawn you have a nice snug little nest.
Good thing Juan is used to being in a confined space

with being on the boat, or he'd feel constricted, don't you think?'

'He hasn't complained yet,' Nora replied, hoping she had not called with the idea of staying for supper. 'I'll fetch my coat.'

Outdoors there was a sweet salty tang in the slight breeze across the water. It was dusk now, throwing the rising moon into relief as it sailed among a peppering of stars. During their walk along the promenade, Tricia prattled on about her activities that day, but Nora hardly listened, although she did manage to make the right rejoinders.

Before they reached the pier the yachts were already rounding the headland, their lights like fireflies in the scented dusk. Nora reckoned that by the time they reached the end of the pier quite a few would be home.

Soon their footsteps were sounding eerily on the boards of the pier and she turned the big collar of her camel coat around her face against the breeze. The yachts were now making for the stone pier and the harbour, with the exception of one which made for the buoys bobbing up and down below them near to the stone steps.

Tricia quickened her steps. 'Finn hasn't won. He's late in,' she said. 'It looks as though we're the only ones on the pier.'

Nora quivered and snuggled deeper into her jacket. The shadows ahead looked menacing, but Juan would soon be there, she thought. There was already a boat tied to one of the buoys near to the pier, but it wasn't the *Dancing Belle*. Then Tricia was running forward to meet the men mounting the steps at the end of the pier. She flung herself into the arms of one of them while the others passed on their way along the pier.

She said, 'Kevin says Juan and Finn are coming

in now—they had trouble around the south of the
island. See you!'

The next moment she had gone with Kevin, leaving Nora staring after them in dismay. So that was
why Tricia had come to the pier—to meet Kevin
Stroud! And now she was all alone on the pier. The
dusk was deepening with every minute. Nora
shivered. The old fears were returning, the fears of
the unknown. Every shadow around her took on
grotesque shapes, every sound was like a pistol shot
to her nerves.

She closed her eyes. 'Come on, please, Juan. Just
come!' she whispered. There were more lights now
coming round the headland and it seemed ages before one of them broke away from the others who
were going further on to the stone pier and the entrance to the harbour.

By the time the party disembarked Nora was
quaking. Regardless of the other men with Juan
she flung herself into his arms.

'Hey now, what's this? What a welcome!' grinned
Juan as he held her tight in his arms. 'With a send-
off like this there's no knowing what we could have
achieved.'

But all Nora heard was the vibration of his voice
in his chest as she buried her face against it. The
sick frightened feeling in her stomach was slowly
departing and it was some seconds before she lifted
her face to his. His embrace was enchanting, his
face cold from the sea air, his mouth warm and urgent. His kiss lingered until she was out of breath,
then he drew her against him and they walked back
along the pier.

Finn had been waiting for them a little distance
away. Nora was walking on air, trying to forget that
Juan had been putting on an act for Finn's benefit.
Flung from such emotional heights it took some

minutes for her to return to normal.

Finn was walking along with them now and Juan was saying,

'All we need now is a good meal after a disappointing day.'

'It's all ready and waiting,' Nora assured him. Then, mindful of what lay ahead, she added. 'And there's plenty for you, Finn, too.'

'I wouldn't dream of intruding,' Finn began half-heartedly.

'Nonsense,' said Juan. 'Of course you'll have a meal with us. You know you're dead on your feet.'

The curtains were drawn in the lounge. The meal had been thoroughly enjoyed and the two men sat back enjoying a cigar. Nora had cleared the dishes away and was preparing to wash them when Juan joined her to help.

'Finn is asleep on the settee,' he said.

As Nora tossed him a tea-towel she felt the need to make one thing clear.

'I hope,' she said, diving into her task industriously and putting the end product on the draining board, 'you didn't think I overdid the welcome back there? As it happened I wasn't exactly enjoying waiting on the pier alone.'

'Then why go?'

She went on to tell him then about Tricia calling and her reason for meeting him. Juan gave a low whistle.

'So she came to meet Kevin Stroud? Interesting,' he mused thoughtfully. 'Anything else happen?'

Nora stared hard at him for several seconds. 'You know,' she said finally, 'we're acting like a couple already married.'

He gave her a look of dark intent. 'We'll come back to that later.'

Nora told him then about Jony coming. 'He

actually blushed when he talked about us.' She giggled. 'It's so funny—Jony romantic, calling Cissy darling, and looking into her eyes.' She leaned against the sink, convulsed. 'He's just lost a cow and I'm sure...he doesn't...he doesn't ...really know whether to get another cow or a wife.'

Paroxysms of laughter convulsed her speech and tears of mirth glistened in her eyes. She wiped them away with a finger, realising that her behaviour was not exactly in keeping with the Nora Bain Juan knew. She sobered on the thought that from now on it was essential to get a hold on herself. She was in a very tricky situation which would become even trickier when Finn had gone, as Juan could do nothing other than stay the night since they were supposed to be married.

If Juan was puzzled over her behaviour he did not show it. He hung up the tea-towel and waited while she rinsed the sink and her hands. He leaned back against the steel structure while she used the hand cream and surveyed her thoughtfully.

'So you enjoyed yourself with Jony? How did he take the wedding announcement?'

'He didn't show it if he was upset. He's bound to be disappointed—all that money within his grasp and then to have only half of it.'

'Did he notice that you had no wedding ring?' His eyes were on her small hands, pink as rose petals. 'Incidentally, you have pretty hands,' he added.

'Thanks,' Nora answered inanely. 'I gave him the impression that it was all to do with keeping the marriage a secret.'

Juan switched off the kitchen light as they moved back into the lounge where they occupied the two comfortable chairs. He stretched out long legs.

'How do you feel about Finn staying the night? He's dead beat and is hardly in a condition to drive himself home. I could take him, but one can hardly refuse a man who gives hospitality himself so freely shelter for the night.' He gave her a steady look as if weighing up her reaction to his suggestion. 'It's for you to say. It's your flat.'

Nora swallowed, visualising more problems ahead. 'But there's only one spare room,' she whispered. 'What about you?'

'I'll be all right,' he said. 'I'd better get him to bed.'

He rose to his feet and went to the settee. It took some time to waken Finn who was flat out, but he managed to get him on his feet and to the guest room. Nora was setting the small dining table for breakfast the following morning when he returned.

'You don't have to do that,' he told her. 'I shall be up early tomorrow morning. Finn will want to go back to The Armitage after breakfast. I've brought my shaving tackle with me, so he can borrow that.'

Nervously, Nora rearranged the place mats on the table.

'Where are you going to sleep?' she asked without looking up.

'I'll use the settee.'

'I'll fetch you a pillow and blankets,' she said.

Juan followed her to the linen cupboard in the small corridor and reached above her head for a spare pillow. He was standing right behind her and Nora found his nearness unbearable.

'I'll get them,' she said illtemperedly. 'For goodness' sake go back into the lounge. The place is like a toy house with you around!'

Juan did not move. He took the pillow and blanket from her, obviously trying to fathom the reason for her outburst.

'I don't expect you to wait upon me even if I do clutter up the place with my size,' he told her quietly as she followed him back to the lounge.

Miserably Nora watched him put the pillow and blanket on the settee.

'I was rude,' she said contritely. 'I'm sorry.'

'Come and sit down. I won't keep you long, then you can go to bed.'

He sat down on the settee and patted the place beside him, but Nora went to sit in one of the chairs.

He gave her a quizzical look. 'Is it any use telling you you have nothing to fear from me staying the night here? I don't take advantage of frightened little girls. I know how scared you were on the pier, but if we're to have some kind of marriage, even if it is only on paper, we have to develop some kind of rapport.'

She twisted her hands in her lap. 'Maybe we ought to forget the whole thing,' she said wretchedly.

'And have ourselves branded as liars? It's too late. I shall buy you a ring while we're in Douglas tomorrow. The whole business, bar mishaps, should be over in a couple of days, then once the will is settled we can set about having the marriage annulled.'

Nora leaned back in her chair and closed her eyes. 'I shall be glad to get back to normal living again minus problems.'

He said cynically, 'My dear girl, you're talking about the impossible. No one can go through life without problems.'

Nora opened her eyes and looked across at him defiantly. 'I didn't seem to have many problems cluttering up the place back home.'

Juan displayed total disbelief. 'Then if that was

so all I can say is that you've never really lived, merely existed.'

'Is that so?' A flicker of annoyance rippled over her face. 'I suppose anyone who doesn't dabble in boats is, by your reckoning, a zombie?'

'I wasn't thinking of boats.' His lips twitched at the sudden colour in her face. 'I was thinking of other things.'

Nora consulted her wrist watch, knowing that her heightened colour was a danger signal. With her voice as steady as she could make it, she said, 'I won't ask you to define those other things at this late hour. I'm off to bed.'

'Just a moment.' Juan spoke with an air of command and Nora's panicky gaze focussed on his tall lean frame as he rose slowly to his feet.

She was scared and she felt he knew it. Her mouth went dry and she was afraid to stand in case her legs gave way. But the need to be normal prevailed and she rose to face him.

His smile did not reach his eyes as his gaze narrowed down to her pale upturned face. His frown told her that he was seeking a reason for her obvious fear.

'You have the kind of eyes that a man can drown in. Do you know that?' he said with a merciless softness. 'Your hair is pure gold in the light and your mouth is like a half opened rose. Furthermore, you're frightened to death of life ... of me.'

Nora took a deep breath and stood her ground. 'I expected something like this when you suggested that Finn should stay the night. I might not have indulged in riotous living, but I can read the signs.'

'Can you indeed?' The dark eyes sparkled with dangerous glints. 'Then let me tell you something, Nora Bain. I was detaining you just now in order to thank you for giving Finn and myself a good meal and shelter for the night, that was all.'

'Oh!' Nora was taken aback. A sense of shame swept
over her. 'I'm sorry,' she said huskily. 'Only you must
admit that in peculiar circumstances one begins to
feel peculiar. It hasn't exactly been a relaxing evening
for me.'

'It hasn't been my day either—or Finn's, for that
matter. I seem to have lost all round,' Juan said
grimly.

The lost race and Tricia? Were they both included
in his lament? Nora quivered.

In lacklustre tones, she whispered, 'And tomorrow?'

'Tomorrow is another day, isn't it?' His laugh was
brief, cynical. 'You might have upset the boat, but life
is never dull. Did I tell you that Richard Garrant is
going to the mainland tomorrow to spend a few days
with his wife before they return? That should give us
time to get things settled.'

Nora paused. 'About the ring—all expenses will
come out of my inheritance, of course.'

She was unprepared for his violent reaction. He
gripped her arms painfully to stare down at her with
a smouldering anger.

'One more crack like that and I'll show you what
you're really missing in life! Now go to bed while I'm
dwelling on what you've done for us this evening.
Goodnight.'

Her released her so suddenly that she fell back
against her chair. The next moment she had slipped
away like a shadow to her room.

For most of the night Nora was weighed down by a
sense of helplessness. She had been buffeted about by
fate. None of the happenings of the day had been of
her own seeking. Neither had the mock marriage to
Juan. She was not forced to go with him to carry it
through. After all, nothing could stop her going

back home and forgetting all about Jed Kelly and his will.

But what about Juan? He had interests here and his livelihood could depend on his integrity, which would take a bashing if she walked out on him now. He was right; they had gone too far to turn back. What a mess!

CHAPTER NINE

NORA awoke on her wedding morning filled with misgivings. As he had promised, Juan had seen to everything and the legalities had been dealt with smoothly. Juan seemed to have the knack of turning everything to his advantage, even to the garden party at Government House to which he was taking her in the afternoon. They were meeting Finn after lunch.

The garden party meant that Nora could attend her wedding in a pretty dress and hat and no one would be any the wiser about their marriage. Her dress, a filmy long-sleeved, uncrushable, washable, white chiffon, mocked her as it hung outside her wardrobe. On a chair nearby was the matching wide-brimmed white lace hat, picot-edged to match the edge of the skirt of her dress.

Well, at least she would look like a bride, she thought, even though she had never felt less like one. The morning had begun on a dull note with low cloud and no sun. It was as gloomy as her thoughts and she would have given anything to be able to talk to someone, to have reassurance that what she was about to do was for the best.

The only bright thought was that it should be as easy to untie the knot of matrimony as it seemed to be to tie it. Was Juan thinking along those lines? He was probably regarding it as just another business deal. And he had done it thoroughly, even to buying her a diamond brooch in the shape of the three legs of Man. She was ready when Juan arrived. For a long moment he stared at her. A gleam came into his dark eyes and was dismissed by a cool smile.

'How are you feeling?' he queried as he handed her into the car. 'You look very garden party-ish. Very nice.'

'As long as I don't look as though I'm going to a wedding,' she answered, borrowing his coolness.

It had not escaped her that he was looking very conservative in a well-cut suit of pale grey with immaculate white silk shirt and sober tie.

He gestured with a well-shaped dark head to the back seat of the car before he started the engine.

'There's a buttonhole there for me and a posy of flowers for you. I thought it safer for us to put them on in the office. Your posy can be left behind to brighten up the room.'

Nora nodded. She was to have no souvenir unless she took one of the flowers from the posy. It was all suddenly very depressing.

She said with a thread of irony, 'There aren't many girls who can regard their first marriage ceremony as a refresher course. Just think, I shall sail through the real thing without a qualm!'

They were turning off the promenade to make for the mountain road and there was a short silence.

'That's one way of looking at it,' answered Juan, putting on speed. 'I'm glad you're not going all coy.'

'Coy?' she cried indignantly. 'I feel just too terrible for words! After all, we are going in for something that's legally binding.'

He said reasonably, 'We aren't actually going in for anything. The situation was forced upon us. My mother used to say, when you enter a bad patch only stay long enough to pick the good out of it. And there's always a bit of good in the worst patches.'

This philosophy did nothing to lift Nora from her gloom.

'And what would you say was the little bit of

good in it for you, since you refuse to consider any payment moneywise?' she asked dryly.

He smiled as though at his own thoughts. 'I'll let you know when we've waded through it. The important thing is that you can settle what you came for and go back home.'

'And the annulment?'

'That can come later. By the way, I have my case in the trunk of the car, my belongings from the Armitage. Aimée was upset because she couldn't go to the garden party.'

'Is Tricia going?'

'No, just Finn and Mr and Mrs Cregeen.' Juan slanted her a grin as she looked at him vacantly for a moment.

'Oh, you mean us?' Nora cried. 'How silly of me!'

'You'll have to get used to it, you know, and quickly.'

She said stiffly, 'I won't let you down.'

'Over your dead body,' he growled. 'Come on, let's have a smile. We're going to be married, not buried!'

The ceremony went without a hitch, two of the staff acting as witnesses. It was over before Nora realised it with only the shining gold band on her finger to prove it.

'Not bad was it?' Juan said as he started the car. 'And now for lunch. I've ordered a table at the Palace restaurant, a corner table with a view of the sea.'

They had champagne and Juan insisted upon addressing her as Mrs Cregeen.

'In case you forget,' he explained.

The day had turned out to be warm and sunny, ideal weather for the garden party. Finn was there in grey suit and topper and congratulated Nora on her pretty dress and hat. They were leaving the grounds of Government House when Juan said casually,

'We're going to the airport to meet a friend of mine. I'm going to ask him to stay the night with us it it's all right with you.'

'At the flat?' Nora gathered her wits at this unexpected announcement, then cried, 'What are we forming, a mutual aid society? If this is a plan to get me into bed with you ...'

'Calm down.' His voice was on ice. 'And don't put ideas into my head. There's a perfectly feasible explanation.'

Nora's voice was on ice. 'There'd better be.'

'Ford Milton is my age, and a lifelong friend. He's Aimée's father. It happened when he was at university—he got drunk one night and Aimée was the result,' he said tightly. 'He didn't marry Tricia. He wasn't the only one she had been with, but the baby was his. He pays for Aimée's keep, but he's been worried lately because she's been unhappy. Tricia has been leaving her more and more on her own or with neighbours.'

'Poor Aimée! What has her father come for? A showdown?' asked Nora, softening.

'No. He wants to take Aimée back home with him for keeps. At the moment he has a contract in California which has twelve more months to run. He reckons that the California sun will do Aimée a lot of good.'

'You think Tricia will let her go?'

'I think so. She's having an affair, and if she's approached while it's white-hot she might just let Aimée go and Kevin might marry her.'

'You mean you wouldn't mind Tricia marrying a cad, which is what this Kevin is in your eyes? That's a bit heartless, isn't it?' she blurted.

'Tricia is heartless, that's why Ford wants to take
Aimée away. At least, if Tricia marries she'll have
security for a while even if it doesn't last, and she's
the kind who'll look after herself.'

'You mean regarding alimony? Charming!' Nora
said caustically.

He said roughly, 'We live in a hard world and you
have to be realistic. Aimée is the important one,
with all her life before her.'

'Is that why you've shown so much interest in
her?'

'All part of the plot,' he answered coolly. 'Ford
has to be convinced that his daughter will be happy
with him. She always has in the time she's spent
with him, but that could have been because of the
treats he gave her. However, Aimée enjoyed my
company as proxy for her father.'

'Did Tricia know of your friendship with Ford?'

'No. It's developed through the years through
business mostly.'

'What exactly do you work for, Juan?' she asked
carefully.

'This and that,' he replied carelessly. 'You don't
have to worry about me. Our business arrangement
is quite sound.'

Nora felt a lump in her throat threatening to
choke her.

'Is that so?' she remarked acidly. 'I'm glad to hear
it.'

He cast her a strange look. 'You don't trust me?'

'Oh, I trust you, but I'm wondering what kind of
man you really are.'

'I'm still the man you met by the pier—or perhaps
I've changed since then, and I'm not sure yet
whether it's a good thing or not.'

'You mean you're more ruthless?' she probed.

'Hell, no. In any case, this isn't the time for postmortems. By the way, Ford isn't married.'

'Which is why you don't want Finn to put him up at the Armitage, where he'd be at the mercy of Tricia and her wiles?'

'That's right,' he conceded. 'The success of the whole operation will depend on the swiftness of its being carried out. Ford is coming armed with the necessary papers and he's having it made legal, so there'll be no reversing the decision when once it's made.'

'Not exactly a compliment to me, is it?' Nora paused to see that they were nearing the airport. 'What about my feminine wiles? Besides, I've always fancied living in California.' She looked at him archly. 'I'm going all coy.'

'Be your age,' he growled, 'and say hello to the fairies. Here comes the Fairy Bridge.'

Nora collapsed into convulsions of merriment. 'Greetings, fairies, from Mr and Mrs Juan Cregeen,' she gasped. 'You see, I remembered. You are funny!'

She mopped the tears of mirth from her eyes as Juan glared at her.

'Define funny,' he snapped.

'Well, first you tell me to grow up, then you tell me to talk to the fairies,' she chuckled.

'Which you did nicely for both of us. Interesting.'

They were at the airport and Juan had taken her elbow as they entered the terminal. Fighting an urge to lean more against him, Nora drew her arm away. Close contact with him only fired her senses for more.

'Why exactly was my greeting to the fairies interesting?' she asked.

He appeared to be considering it. 'You replied for both of us, which was very comforting since you appeared to have my interests at heart,' he mocked.

'Don't kid yourself,' she answered, sore at his obvious carefree attitude. Did he never take anything seriously? 'As a matter of fact, I was establishing our new identity, which was only polite. Not that I think they would approve of it.'

'So you don't care if the fairies have it in for me?'

'Poor you! I can just see you cowering behind a bush.' Nora craned her neck as she heard a plane landing on the runway. 'What time is your friend arriving?'

Juan glanced at his watch. 'That could be him.'

It was. Ford Milton was not much to look at—medium height, brown hair and nice grey eyes which focussed you directly behind dark-rimmed spectacles. Studious type, mused Nora, and was not sure. She certainly could not see him being seduced by Tricia. But much water had gone under the bridge since then. He was much too mild to be Tricia's type, but he did look prosperous in his expensive city-going suit which he filled nicely.

His smile, however, lighted up his features very attractively. His greeting was warm, his gaze at Nora said, 'Wow.'

During the drive back to the flat Juan put him right on recent events and by the time the journey was over Ford seemed to be more relaxed. Nora had bought extra supplies in case of emergency and cooked a meal for them. While it was cooking she put clean bed linen on the bed in the spare room, leaving the two men talking together in the lounge over a drink.

A telephone call from Floyd came as she was about to sit down to supper. He insisted upon knowing the date she proposed to return.

'Give me a ring tomorrow,' she answered. 'I'm busy right now.'

She felt mean not telling Floyd about her marriage, but there would be no need to go into details if it was soon to be annulled. A great depression that had begun with her falling over Juan's suitcase in her bedroom quenched her appetite.

'Come on, you're eating nothing,' Juan urged. 'Don't you like your own cooking?'

'Not hungry,' she said with a smile at Ford's concerned regard. 'Too much sun at the garden party this afternoon.'

'Headache?' Juan asked.

'A bit muzzy, but it will pass,' she admitted.

He raised a dark brow. 'Cissy? She might be good for a sedative if she's in the building.'

'No, thanks,' she said firmly. 'It will pass.'

'Nice little place you have here,' Ford commented over coffee.

'Nora's,' Juan said laconically.

'Very nice. It's kind of you, Nora, to have me here. I won't inconvenience you for longer than I can help,' Ford told her with a smile. To Juan, he said, 'Are you sure this lawyer, Richard Garrant, will come tomorrow?'

Juan nodded. 'He's just returned from the mainland and will be here tomorrow afternoon.'

'Good. Let's hope Tricia comes up to expectations.' Ford had the look of a man watching a dark cloud on its way. 'You see, there's this girl in California. I like her a lot, but I haven't said anything to her until she sees Aimée.'

Nora felt her coffee would choke her. Juan's best friend, and he was deceiving him about their marriage. To be fair there was nothing Juan could do about it since it was only a business arrangement making it his own concern. All the same, she felt she had to get away from pretence, so she left them talking and went to bed.

She fell over Juan's suitcase again and gave it a

vicious kick, which didn't help because she stubbed her toe most painfully. She did not need spectacles to see why he had left it in the way. It was to remind her that he had the right of access to her room even though there was no room for him to put his clothes.

With so much on her mind it was not surprising that Nora did not sleep. She lay wide-eyed waiting for them to go to bed. After what seemed years there was a low murmur of voices in the corridor, then silence. She had been lying on her back and drifting off to sleep when there was a movement beside her bed.

Turning in the dim light, she saw the powerful shoulders and broad chest of Juan bending over her. She pushed herself up on her elbow in horror, then swallowed convulsively to see that the bare manly chest tapered down into white shorts.

He was holding a cup of steaming liquid. 'Coffee is not good to go to sleep on, so I brought you a warm drink to send you off,' he whispered, then stopped short at the look on her face. 'What's the matter?'

'You...you...I...I...' Nora began, and could not go on.

His look of consternation turned to amusement. He put the cup down on the bedside table.

'You thought I was nude, didn't you...that I'd come in to get in bed with you?'

Furiously Nora hit out at him, pushing herself up in bed to do so.

'You wanted me to think that, didn't you?' she cried furiously. 'Having a good laugh at my expense?'

He sat down on the bed beside her and caught her hands in a firm grip. 'Stop it!' he hissed. 'Do you want Ford to hear?'

But Nora was in no mood for discretion. 'What do I care if he hears or not? You ... you naked ape!'

Juan put a hand over her mouth. 'Idiot!' he whispered, then drew in a deep breath as she set her teeth in his hand.

The next moment he had pushed her back on the bed and his mouth closed on her own punishingly. She writhed and struggled, but it made no difference. The kiss went on and on until she had no further resistance, and gradually her fingers slipped their hold on his hair.

His voice was a trifle thick as he raised his head. 'Another peep from you and you'll get it again— and you know what that will lead to, don't you?' he warned. 'Now have your drink and go to sleep like a good little girl.'

He had gone before she realised it and she closed her eyes with the taste of blood on her lips. Was it blood from her own mouth which he had crushed against her teeth or was it from biting his hand? Nora was too confused to know. She only knew that it was mingling with the salt of tears raining down her face, and the taste was very bitter indeed.

Tricia came to the flat the next morning. Juan fetched her from The Armitage and Nora went out shopping, leaving them together. Juan had dropped Tricia off at the flats and had gone off somewhere himself. Nora dreaded meeting him again. He had gone out to fetch Tricia when she got up, and what Ford told her at breakfast did not make her feel any better.

Juan, it seemed, was a director of several firms dealing in components for ships, aircraft and motor vehicles. He had come to the island at Ford's request to help him get his daughter.

'Juan's a grand person,' Ford told her, 'I'd trust him with my life. I knew that in order to get

Aimée Tricia would have to get involved with a
man who wouldn't want the responsibility of
another man's child, so when Finn invited her here
I hoped it would lead to something.'

Nora hoped it would. She arrived back at the
flat to find Tricia smoking a cigarette and Ford
watchful.

'Staying to lunch, aren't you, Tricia?' she asked.

Tricia regarded her with hard eyes. 'I'll think
about it,' she said sharply.

'I should,' replied Nora coolly. 'Everybody feels
better with a good meal inside them.'

Ford gave her a grateful look and Nora set about
preparing food. Juan came in around midday with
Richard Garrant, and as the dining table only
seated four, he perched on a high stool from the
kitchen. The meal prepared generously for four of
them left ample for Richard Garrant who, Nora had
understood, was coming after lunch. He was, however, going somewhere else in the afternoon, so they
got down to business while Nora washed the dishes,
helped by Juan.

There was no opportunity for either of them to
say anything without being overheard by the others
in the lounge, and Nora evaded Juan's eyes.

Before the legal adoption proceedings got under
way Richard Garrant insisted upon seeing Aimée in
order for her to make her own choice of parent. Juan
went to fetch her and since she arrived with her suitcase it appeared the choice had already been made.
Aimée was going with her father. In fact she insisted upon sitting on his knee during the whole
proceedings.

Tricia made no fuss. She accepted the very generous cheque which Ford gave her and signed away
all claim to her daughter. As she was going to
marry without the encumbrance of a growing

daughter, Tricia was quite amiable and unruffled.

Tricia left first. Then Ford left with Aimée to stay at a hotel in Douglas before leaving for the first stage of their journey to California the next morning.

Richard Garrant shook his head sadly when they had gone.

'I hate to take on a case like this,' he confessed. 'But I do admire the man for facing up to his responsibilities towards his own child. I must say I preferred him to the young woman. And now for something more pleasant.'

He favoured Juan and Nora with a paternal smile. 'If I can have your marriage certificate and the other documents, we can have this settled in no time.'

He smiled at Juan, who was leaning negligently against the door frame having come back from seeing Ford and Aimée off.

'Sorry you didn't win the yacht race, Juan, but you can't win every time. I suppose you will be leaving us soon?'

'That's right,' agreed Juan. 'I'd like you to sew the loose ends up as quickly as you can.'

'I'll do that. It should be plain sailing anyway. I'd like to wish you both a great deal of happiness.'

They thanked him politely, Nora avoiding Juan's eyes. But she did look at him when he said, 'Can I drop you anywhere, Richard? I'm going to see Finn.'

'No, thanks. I have my car,' Juan replied.

He left with Richard, leaving Nora wandering aimlessly around the flat pondering on his next move. His suitcase had been removed from her bedroom into the guest room, and she wandered into it to gaze at the single bed. The bed in her room was a double one—whether by accident or design she

would never know, but the firm who furnished the
flat would have set it out in the conventional way.

It took her two minutes to make up her mind to
move Juan's things into her room before moving
hers into his. At least she would be more comfortable in a single bed than he would. He came
around seven o'clock with a huge box of groceries
and some rainbow trout freshly caught.

'Fancy some trout for supper?' he asked.

Nora had taken care with her clothes and had
dressed for dinner that evening.

She said, 'I was about to go out for dinner.'

He lifted a provocative dark brow. 'No rainbow
trout? I can recommend it. Cooked my way, of
course.'

'Of course.'

Juan cooked the fish while Nora laid the table.
There were two bottles of champagne in the box of
groceries and she put one on ice. She made the
sauce for the fish, put out a chunk of cheese from
the grocery box Juan had bought and a plate of
savoury biscuits. Her appetite was nil, but Juan
would undoubtedly enjoy his meal and he could fill
up with the cheese and biscuits.

The fish was delicious, but it was like sawdust in
Nora's mouth. His dark eyebrows climbed a little
as she played about with her portion of fish, but he
said nothing. He did, however, put a generous portion of cheese on her plate.

'I can't eat all that!' she cried, aghast.

'You can if you try. You talked earlier of going
out to dinner, so eat!'

He filled her glass with champagne several times
and Nora had kept drinking it to wash down food
she had no appetite for. The result was that she was
a trifle tipsy at the end of the meal. She kept giggling and did not know why.

Juan made the coffee and put on the radio to listen to a concert. Nora got up and danced around the room to the dreamy tune. Juan said nothing. He smoked a cigar, then followed her into the kitchen when she drifted in to wash the dishes. Still giggling, she reached up to put a cup on his head. He took it off, swept her up bodily in his arms and carried her to her room where he put her down on the bed.

'You'd better sleep it off,' he told her, bending down to slip off her shoes.

Nora's expression was one of indignant surprise. 'Thanks,' she cried. 'And don't thank me for giving you the best ... the best ... bedroom in the flat!'

He narrowed a dark-eyed glance at her. 'Disappointed, are you, that I didn't come up to expectations?'

For a moment she blinked uncomprehendingly, then she got his meaning. The colour beat in her cheeks as anger knotted in her throat.

'Why, you beast!' she exclaimed furiously. 'You big conceited oaf! Did you actually believe I'd taken your things to my room with the object of sharing my bed with you? Get out!'

Bending down, she picked up one of her shoes and threw it with all her might at him. It struck the door as he closed it.

Nora was up early the next morning. From her window the beach looked inviting as the tide slowly receded, and the next minute she was going quietly from the flat for an early morning swim. On her return she was going to book her flight home.

There was nothing to be gained in staying. She was going to put an ocean between herself and the aggravating man who could arouse such a terrible ache of longing in her breast. A man who could appraise her with such cool appraisal was hardly likely to be in love with her. In his own eyes he was very much a superior male. In hers he was a male chauvinist of the worst kind.

She was building up her antagonism against him when she noticed that the *Dancing Belle* was no longer at her moorings at the pier. What did she care that it was another sign that Juan would soon be leaving too? But she had to go first, if only to save her pride.

Juan was out when she returned to the flat. The table was set for her breakfast and the morning newspaper was by her plate. She was having her coffee when the postman came with an invitation from Jony and Cissy to their engagement party in two days' time. She was glad Jony had decided to follow her advice and approach Cissy before his house-keeper left him on his own.

She went to the airport to book a flight at the earliest possible date, thinking she could be lucky in getting a cancelled seat. But she had two days to wait before she could fly off the island. She spent the day in Douglas and arrived back at her flat to find Juan cooking the evening meal. She had left Jony's invitation on the table where he would see it, but he made no comment.

They were polite to each other, leaving Nora at a loss on how to deal with Juan's big-brother attitude. After dinner he went out and when he returned with the spare key she had given him, she was in bed. The last two days had simply crawled for Nora, but soon she would be going home.

It was Jony's engagement party the next evening, but she did not intend to go on her own and Juan had said nothing about it. So she was surprised when he came in early to ask her why she was not dressing for the party.

With her departure getting nearer she left discretion to the winds and told him that she wasn't going.

'Why not?' he demanded. 'Jony had made a very friendly gesture in inviting us, since our marriage has done him out of a great deal of money.'

'So what?' she answered rudely. 'It's all perfectly legal? Besides, he has enough.'

'That isn't the point. We're going whether you like it or not.'

Juan went to his room to change and when he was ready he found Nora still in the lounge flicking over the pages of a magazine.

Without a word, he took the magazine away and scooping her up into his arms strode with her to put her down in her bedroom.

'Now get changed or I'll do it for you,' he warned.

For minutes after he had gone Nora stood and thought it over. Then deciding that going out was better than staying in with him, she began to change.

The party was being held at the farmhouse. 'Trust Jony not to go to the expense of a hotel,' said Juan as he set his car in motion.

Nora turned her head to study his profile. 'This will be our last outing together,' she told him.

He gave her a somewhat startled glance. 'How come?' he asked curiously.

'That would be tellling,' she answered, refusing to be drawn by changing the topic of conversation. 'So the *Dancing Belle* has gone? Has Finn gone too?'

'Yes,' laconically.

'Which leaves you. Are you taking me to Jony's party to let it be known that we really are married?'

'Maybe.'

'Why didn't you leave with Finn?' she asked curiously.

'Why Finn? He's just a friend. I didn't come over

with him. What are you getting at?' They were on a long stretch of straight tree-lined road and he cast her a frown.

'Only that you could have been using him as you've used me to fit in with your own plans.'

Juan said coolly, 'Since I stand to gain nothing with you I fail to see why you should think I've been using you.'

Nora stared down at the bright gold band on her finger which never ought to have been put there in the first place.

'What exactly do you want, Juan?' she whispered huskily.

'I want what you want, to get the whole thing straightened out and completed so we...I'm free to leave it all behind.'

'I see,' she answered, but she did not see. 'It hasn't exactly been a carefree visit, has it?'

Her voice held a note of strain and he flicked her a wary look.

'I wouldn't say that. It's had its compensations.'

For you perhaps, but not for me, she thought unhappily. One thing she had discovered was that money did not always bring happiness except in material comforts. Juan had cruised along at a purring speed, knowing exactly where Jony's farm was and drawing up eventually through double gates and along an earth path with a rectangle of barns to his left and the house to his right.

Jony and Cissy greeted them and they were escorted into a homely lounge where they met the other guests and were presented with a drink. There were about a dozen people in all whom Nora had never met before, but Juan appeared to know them quite well. It was Juan's charm and personality which carried them through the evening and the other guests put her few responses to their questions down to shyness—at least Nora hoped so.

Juan proposed the toast to the happy couple and Jony in reply let it be known that the party was also a farewell to his housekeeper who was leaving him at the end of the month to go to reside with her sister on the mainland. He caught Nora's eye as he said it and his smile was wholly for her.

On the way home in the car they were extremely polite to each other, Nora almost completely silent and speaking only when she had to. She had been too wretched to realise at the farm that it had once been Jed Kelly's home and there had been so much she had wanted to see which would bring the personality of the man closer. Now she would never know, since she had no intention of ever coming to the island again. It would be too painful. She could rent the flat until she decided what to do with it.

Back in the flat she announced that she was going to bed, then paused, realising that it was probably the last time she would see Juan since she was going the next morning while he was out. Her plane did not leave until noon. But he did not look at her and she walked slowly to her room.

But going to bed was one thing, going to sleep was another. The lump in her chest might have been indigestion by the way it insisted on swelling—her own fault for forcing herself to eat food when she had nurtured no appetite for it.

In the end she decided to get up and make a warm drink. Her watch said three o'clock, so there was no likelihood of Juan being up.

Flitting noiselessly to the kitchen, Nora put some milk into a pan and stared at it unseeingly while she waited for it to heat up. She had to keep blinking away the tears that blurred her vision as events crowded in on her which somehow began to be unbearable. Unreasonably she found herself blaming Jed Kelly's will for bringing her unhappiness. If it had not been for Jed she would not have met Juan, she would not be in the impossible position she was now in, and she certainly would not have been feeling unhappy.

The milk boiled over and she mopped it up before trailing back to her room with what was left of the milk. But by the time she had reached her room she felt the lump in her throat too constricting for her to attempt to swallow the drink. Putting it down on the table, she crumpled on her bed and wept.

Her pent-up emotions came out in a flood of tears. With her face buried in her pillow she gave way to her utter misery. So upset was she that it was some moments before she heard the peremptory tap on the door.

'Are you all right, Nora?' Juan called. 'There's a smell of burning. What's going on?'

Nora tried to stop a dry sob being audible. 'Go away! I was heating some milk and it boiled over,' she cried.

'Are you ill?' The next moment he was in the room, taking in her recumbent form and the cup of milk on the bedside table. 'My poor sweet!' he said, sitting down on the bed and touching her shoulder.

Nora's reaction was to burrow her face deeper into her pillow.

'Go away,' she repeated.

'I know how you're feeling,' he said, turning her over gently on her back. 'I had a touch of indigestion myself earlier on.' He smiled. 'I didn't feel like eating much myself at Jony's this evening.'

Nora forgot that her face was blotched and shiny with weeping. If it did not hurt so much it would really be funny. She wanted to tell him so much of her love for him and he was putting her distress down to indigestion! Despairingly she laid an arm across her eyes.

'Go away!' she wailed. 'Please go away.'

Juan pushed the bright hair damp with sweat from her hot forehead gently.

'My poor sweet! I can't call Cissy for help this time,' he said in gentle tones. 'But ...'

Suddenly it was all too much for poor Nora. With a violent movement she swept his hand away.

'Damn Cissy, damn you, damn everybody!' she cried furiously. 'Get out and leave me alone!'

For one terrifying breathless moment she saw his face harden, the dark eyes probe her distorted face. Then his mouth lifted at the corners as he bent his head to claim her mouth. His arms went around her and as the magic got through to her Nora gave herself up to the ecstasy of being kissed hungrily and passionately by Juan. When at last he could tear himself away from her lips he moved his mouth to the side of her neck and groaned.

'My poor sweet! I'm just begining to realise the kind of thing you've been going through, something that can't be cured by bicarb. I've been in a little private hell myself these last few days wondering what on earth had happened to me. While I've been on the island I've been trying to clinch a deal with a millionaire who's interested in our products.'

He raised eyes dark with need and smiled down at her sadly.

'The way I went about it scared me. I'm sure the man looked at me as some kind of nut who'd got where I am in the business world through sheer luck. I kept calling him Nora—which goes to show how far gone I am about you.'

He was kissing her neck, his lips moving down

urgently into softer flesh. Nora lay perfectly still
as his words got through to her. She was dreaming,
of course. It was not true. But the weight of his
hard body was true enough, so were his lips. And
her heart was beating loud enough to wake her from
the deepest sleep.

He went on, 'What I'm trying to say, my sweet, is
that I love you to distraction.' He lifted his head
again to gaze down tenderly into her bewildered
face. 'Not putting this very well, am I? I can do it
much better this way.'

And indeed he did. Nora simply had to return his
kisses in a delirium of happiness. It was a long time
before he gave way to the pressure of her hands on
his chest.

'You've guessed that ... I love you, haven't you?'
she gasped on breath regained.

'Now I have. Why didn't you let me know before?' he demanded. 'The state I've been in since
we returned from Jony's place! I undressed and
lay on the top of the bed, restraining myself from
coming in to you. One move from you and I was
sunk. I thought I heard you go to the kitchen, then
I smelled the overspill of milk on the cooker and
thought you were ill.'

Nora said unsteadily, 'You aren't feeling sorry for
me, are you, because you know how I feel about
you?'

'Hell, no! I've been feeling too sorry for myself.
I love you so much that I've had nightmares about
losing you. I forced you to go to Jony's party with
the idea that some of their happiness would soften
you towards me. Now tell me why you were crying.'

She touched his face tenderly, lovingly. 'I was
crying because I love you and you couldn't seem to
care less. All that stuff about not wanting to see the
same face at breakfast each morning. And you were

so sure you were happy as you were?'

'I am happy—very happy—as your husband.'

Nora had to lower her eyes from the look in his. 'But you always treated me like Aimée,' she whispered. 'I suppose it will take some time for us to... adjust ourselves to...marriage?'

He grinned at her heightened colour, and kissed her nose.

'A terrible long time. As long as it takes me to carry you to your own room—our room.'

He was suddenly teasing and vital. All the old arrogance was back as he scooped her bodily into his arms and bore her away.

It was a long time later when Nora reluctantly stirred herself in the curve of his arm as he lay beside her.

'I hope you don't really believe I gave you this room with the ulterior motive of sharing it with you?' she said.

Juan chuckled. 'Talking about ulterior motives! I deliberately got you drunk the other evening on champagne to get you into bed with me. But I told myself that I didn't want you that way. You had to love me as much as I love you.'

He pulled her into his arms. 'I've another confession to make—I cancelled your flight back home. The airport rang up on the day you'd gone there. It was just before you returned to the flat in the evening. There was a cancellation for the next day.'

'You double-crosser!' she cried. 'Whatever shall I do with you?'

'I'll show you,' he murmured, stifling her soft laugh with the passionate pressure of his lips. He did in the nicest possible way and her arms slid around his neck in complete capitulation.

Harlequin Romances

The books that let you escape
into the wonderful world of romance!
Trips to exotic places…interesting
plots…meeting memorable people…
the excitement of love….These are
integral parts of Harlequin Romances –
the heartwarming novels read by
women everywhere.

Many early issues are now available.
Choose from this great selection!

Choose from this list of Harlequin Romance editions.*

*Some of these book were originally published under different titles.

Relive a great love story…
Harlequin Romances 1980
Complete and mail this coupon today!

Harlequin Reader Service

In U.S.A.
MPO Box 707
Niagara Falls, N.Y. 14302

In Canada
649 Ontario St.
Stratford, Ontario, N5A 6W2

Please send me the following Harlequin Romance novels. I am enclosing my check or money order for $1.25 for each novel ordered, plus 59¢ to cover postage and handling.

☐ 422	☐ 509	☐ 636	☐ 729	☐ 810	☐ 902
☐ 434	☐ 517	☐ 673	☐ 737	☐ 815	☐ 903
☐ 459	☐ 535	☐ 683	☐ 746	☐ 838	☐ 909
☐ 481	☐ 559	☐ 684	☐ 748	☐ 872	☐ 920
☐ 492	☐ 583	☐ 713	☐ 798	☐ 878	☐ 927
☐ 508	☐ 634	☐ 714	☐ 799	☐ 888	☐ 941

Number of novels checked @ $1.25 each = $_____

N.Y. State residents add appropriate sales tax $_____

Postage and handling $_____ .59

TOTAL $_____

I enclose _____
(Please send check or money order. We cannot be responsible for cash sent through the mail.)

Prices subject to change without notice.

NAME _____
(Please Print)

ADDRESS _____

CITY _____

STATE/PROV. _____

ZIP/POSTAL CODE _____

Offer expires March 31, 1981

01256337